MYSTERY OF THE TEMPEST

A Fisher Key Adventure

Advance Praise for *Mystery of the Tempest*

"*Mystery of the Tempest* is brilliantly conceived and executed. The characters literally jump off the page and into your heart. A funny, thrilling, authentic young adult novel in the Fisher Key Adventure series. I can't wait for the next installment."—Julie Anne Peters, author of *Luna* and *Keeping You a Secret*

"Danger, mystery, suspense, romance, conflict, and teen angst woven into a plot that speeds along complete with crackling dialogue— what more could a reader want? You'll be hooked from the tense opening scene, and after you turn the last page, you'll eagerly await the sequel. Sam Cameron's writing is a gift to teens, past and present. Thoroughly enjoyable."—Lesléa Newman, author of *Heather Has Two Mommies* and *A Letter to Harvey Milk*

"In the spirit of the mystery series I used to devour as a kid, and yet, so different and so much better—contemporary, diverse, populated with believable people, fresh, fun, funny, and actually kind of brilliant…"—Kristin Cashore, author of *Graceling* and *Fire*

"Intrigue that will delight genre enthusiasts: explosions, competing investigations, false identities…and a harrowing climax."—*Kirkus Reviews*

Acclaim for Bold Strokes Books Soliloquy Titles

Speaking Out: LGBTQ Youth Stand Up edited by Steve Berman

"Speaking Out offers gay youth a valuable and unique insight into what it means to be gay in America and how there's nothing wrong with being proud of it. As a young gay man myself, I found it extremely powerful, and highly recommend it to any young LGBT person who seeks to find more answers about the gay identity and community as a whole."—James Duke Mason, actor and youth activist

Mesmerized by David-Matthew Barnes

"Barnes' young adult novel about two boys suddenly, deeply in love has a fairy-tale tone, but it will strike all the right notes for YA readers as the boys dance into the hearts of The Showdown audience."—Richard Labonte, *Book Marks*

Cursebusters! by Julie Smith

"Smith's first young adult novel is funny and filled with heart. ... Smith offers a lively adventure story packed with New Age mystery and magic, and moments of heart-stopping suspense. Teens who enjoy this novel will be hoping for a sequel."—*VOYA*

Who I Am by M.L. Rice

"Ms. Rice has written a beautiful YA novel which deals with high-school pressures, bullies, coming out to friends and family, and the overwhelming feelings of falling in love for the first time. Devin is a funny and engaging character and you really feel her happiness, pain, sorrow, and love (and the thousand other emotions teenagers go through in the span of 10 minutes). Ms. Rice has an excellent way of showing the scary and thrilling experiences and feelings of coming out, as well as dealing with both the positive and negative reactions a person can receive upon doing so. A great book for teenagers (and adults alike)!"—*Bibliophilic Book Blog*

Sleeping Angel by Greg Herren

"…It [Sleeping Angel] will probably be put on the young adult (YA) shelf, but the fact is that it's a cracking good mystery that general readers will enjoy as well. It just happens to be about teens…A unique viewpoint, a solid mystery and good characterization all conspire to make Sleeping Angel a welcome addition to any shelf, no matter where the bookstores stock it."—Jerry Wheeler, *Out in Print*

The Perfect Family by Kathryn Shay

"This well-written book is noteworthy at a time when the suicide of gay teens has been in the news. It illustrates the conflicting psychological and varying religious perspectives on homosexuality and shows that support can be found in communities and with straight allies. It could be invaluable in helping to encourage a dialogue among families going through similar events. The story includes frank talk about suicides and things that parents should be attuned to notice. The pace is engaging but not overly dramatic, providing a realistic journey for any reader."—Bob Lind, *Echo Magazine*

"The image of the 'perfect' family is shattered when the youngest son announces he's gay and it's going to take more than glue to patch it back together. Warmly poignant, realistic, dramatic and honestly presented, Shay's story is an engrossing family saga for the modern world…4.5 stars."—Pat Cooper, *Romantic Times Book Reviews*

Father Knows Best by Lynda Sandoval

"In classic YA style, Sandoval works potent messages into her plot: gay is good, marriage ought to be for everyone and eschewing sex can be cool. Sound advice—and Sandoval delivers it without a scintilla of preachiness in this snappy, cheerfully snarky novel about girl power and powerful friendships."—*OutFront Colorado*

365 Days by KE Payne

"YA novel or not, 365 Days absofreakinlutely blew me away. The writing is crisp and clever; the characters are simple yet multi-dimensional; and the storyline is fresh but familiar. Ms. Payne artfully captures the confusion and concerns of a young woman coming to terms with her lesbian libido, as well as life with her family, the inconvenience of schoolwork, morphing dynamics with friends, the torment of waiting for a text, an email, or a call, and the near-consuming fear of losing it all."—*The Rainbow Reader*

Visit us at www.boldstrokesbooks.com

MYSTERY OF THE TEMPEST

A Fisher Key Adventure

by

Sam Cameron

2011

MYSTERY OF THE TEMPEST: A FISHER KEY ADVENTURE

ISBN 10: 1-60282-579-3
ISBN 13: 978-1-60282-579-6

This Trade Paperback Original Is Published By
Bold Strokes Books, Inc.
P.O. Box 249
Valley Falls, NY 12185

First Edition: November 2011

CREDITS
EDITORS: Greg Herren and Cindy Cresap
PRODUCTION DESIGN: Susan Ramundo
COVER DESIGN BY SHERI (GRAPHICARTIST2020@HOTMAIL.COM)

Dedication

For the boys

CHAPTER ONE

Trapped thirty feet below the surface of the shimmering Atlantic, his right foot caught in the wreck of a sunken ship, Denny Anderson thought: *I'm going to die.*

I'm going to die a virgin, he amended.

An eighteen-year-old virgin.

An eighteen-year-old virgin who was supposed to graduate high school in—he checked his black dive watch—two hours.

Denny could see the headline in the *Fisher Key Gazette: Local Teen Perishes in Underwater Tragedy.* The newspaper would run a photo of him, or Steven, or both of them together. It didn't matter, since most people couldn't tell them apart. The article would highlight his academic and sports achievements at Fisher Key High—more academic than sports, since he usually left the jock stuff to Steven—and talk about his acceptance to the Coast Guard Academy. Maybe there'd even be a paragraph or two about how he and Steven had often helped their father, Captain Greg Anderson of the sheriff's office, solve local crimes and save the occasional life or two.

Would be nice if he could save his own, though.

Denny yanked again on his trapped foot. The *Manitowoc* was an old cutter that had been sunk to create an artificial reef just a few miles off Fisher Key. The Florida Keys already had the third biggest reef system in the world, but the boat was a special treat—already blooming with plants and sea life, swarmed by yellow and blue tangs. Before sinking it, the Coast Guard had stripped off any cables, lines, or other diving hazards to make the wreck.

But underwater relics tended to shift and change in the strong currents, and storms could upset them as well. A railing near the stern had collapsed onto Denny's foot as he was swimming past an open hatch.

He checked his tank. Twenty minutes of air left.

Hello, Steven, he thought. *Where are you?*

No sign of his twin. Probably at the bow, snapping photos with the new camera their grandparents had sent as a graduation gift.

Maybe Steven would use it to take pictures at Denny's funeral.

Stop with the drama, he told himself. He twisted around and tugged again on the collapsed railing. He didn't have enough leverage to get himself free. Too bad he didn't have any convenient crowbars.

But he could *make* one.

He stretched out to the end of the collapsed rail, braced his free foot at an old weld, and started pulling. The metal had weakened, but it didn't snap free. He tugged some more, thinking hard about all he still needed to accomplish in his life: get laid, fall in love, share a passionate kiss.

Not necessarily in that order.

Steven had nailed all three of those, spectacularly, by the time he was sixteen. Not that Denny was keeping score. Okay, of course he was keeping score. But it was easier for Steven. He had the confidence and ambition to do anything he wanted. Like the whole SEAL thing. Since age twelve, Steven had set his dreams on being a Navy SEAL. On the day that Denny got his acceptance letter from the Coast Guard, Steven had driven up to Miami and enlisted. No problem. He liked to brag that by the time Denny graduated, Steven would already have saved people on top secret missions around the world.

Denny considered himself to be confident and ambitious as well, but the key difference between their love lives was biological and irreversible.

Steven liked girls.

Denny liked boys.

Huge difference.

Not that Denny couldn't have kissed a guy if he'd wanted to. He didn't want to.

Couldn't want to.

Not until he graduated from the Coast Guard Academy. Don't ask, don't tell, and don't get discharged.

A shadow passed over him. Denny looked up and saw exactly what he didn't want to see: the sleek outline of a nurse shark, looking for lunch.

Eaten by a shark. So not his idea of a good time—or a good death.

He stopped trying to free himself and waited for the beast to pass. It meandered over him for a moment, as if toying with him, and swam north. Once it was gone, Denny checked his air again. Fourteen minutes left.

Thirteen.

Twelve.

Finally, a piece of railing snapped free. He wedged it beside his trapped foot and applied some careful pressure. He freed himself just as Steven swam into view, blissfully ignorant of how close he'd come to being an only child.

Steven jerked his thumb toward the surface. *Time to go.*

Denny kicked upward with his flippers and rose through the shimmering blue water.

When they surfaced, the sky was a flat, cloudless blue. Gorgeous. Everything about the Florida Keys was beautiful to Denny. If there was anything he wasn't looking forward to about the Academy, it was New London's dreary winters and the cold waters of Long Island Sound.

Steven spat out his mouthpiece and reached for the side of their dinghy. "We've got an audience."

Denny twisted in the water. Bobbing on the waves nearby was a crappy old fishing boat in desperate need of a paint job. She seemed barely seaworthy. Standing on her deck, however, was a Greek god of a man. Tall, chiseled, golden-haired. Impossibly handsome. Late twenties? Early thirties at the most. Muscled arms with a broad chest and narrow waist, barely clothed in a pair of white shorts. He was better looking than any man Denny had ever ogled online or in real life.

Denny wanted to leap out of the water and tackle him with a big kiss.

The whole virginity problem could be solved by this man, on the deck of that old boat, in just a few minutes.

"How's the diving, boys?" the Greek god asked.

Steven looked unimpressed by the stranger's good looks. He hauled himself into the dinghy and said, "It's okay."

"This is where they sank that cutter, right?" the man asked.

Denny wanted to contribute something to the conversation—anything at all. Preferably, something to prove how suave and intelligent he was. He just knew he'd do the exact opposite if he opened his mouth.

Steven squinted at the man. "You shouldn't dive alone. It's dangerous."

The man laughed. "I think I can handle it."

Denny was sure he could.

The man's gaze lifted up to something in the water behind Denny. "There's a beauty."

Still treading water, Denny twisted around. A seventy-foot wooden sailing yacht sailed majestically past them on a course for Fisher Key. All five of her sails were hoisted to catch the steady wind. Denny had been around sailboats, yachts, launches, and other boats all his life, and he even owned his own speedboat, but this ship was completely out of his class. Some kind of antique racing boat, he figured.

They couldn't see her crew, but Steven read the ship's name from her stern. "*The Tempest*. Shakespeare crap."

The yacht headed proudly toward shore.

"Come on," Steven said, ready to start the engine. "Mom'll kill us if we're late."

They wished the man happy diving and steered toward home. As the Greek god grew smaller and disappeared behind them, Denny felt exactly like a lovesick thirteen-year-old.

"Stop drooling," Steven said, looking stormy. "He wasn't that handsome."

"He was drop-dead gorgeous."

"You're pathetic. How are you going to fool anyone at the academy if you drool over any guy who wanders by?"

"Who asked you for advice?" Denny demanded.

"I'm just saying."

"You've been pissy all week. For someone who's going to graduate with honors and then go deflower Kelsey—"

"No one calls it 'deflowering' anymore, you idiot. And it's none of your business."

"She's told everyone at school! I think I saw it online, too."

"Shut up."

Denny studied Steven's profile in the glare of sunlight. Twin or not, you couldn't share your whole life with someone and not know when something was bothering them. Steven's crankiness made it seem like he was dreading graduation rather than looking forward to it.

Getting Steven to admit anything was always a major chore. He wasn't just a closed book. He was a closed, locked, shrink-wrapped book buried in a treasure chest at the bottom of the deep blue ocean.

Considering the day he'd had so far, Denny didn't feel like trying to pry open that treasure chest anytime soon.

"You're the idiot," he muttered. He couldn't see the Greek god anymore, but he was out there somewhere. Waiting on the horizon. For the rest of the trip he fantasized about the Greek god sailing around the world with him on a beautiful yacht.

A boy could dream, couldn't he?

CHAPTER TWO

S tanding in the crowded, sunlit band room of Fisher Key High School, Steven felt sick. Some of that came from the rum and Coke that Eddie Ibarra had been passing around in the parking lot until just a few minutes ago. Eddie was always stealing alcohol from his mother. In the Secret Yearbook in Steven's head, Eddie had already been nominated as both (a) Most Likely to Have a DUI, and (b) Most Likely to End Up in Rehab.

Which sucked, because they'd been friends for twelve years, and Steven didn't know how to save Eddie from the bad road ahead.

Most of the twisty feeling in Steven's gut, however, came from knowing he'd already screwed up his own life and had no right to advise anyone else.

Not even the absolute certainty of sex with Kelsey Carlson tonight could cheer him up.

"You look green," Kelsey said, straightening his tie for him. She was gorgeous in her yellow dress, her blond hair curled in dozens of ringlets. She'd dabbed herself with some exotic Indian perfume, and it was strongest from the vee between her ample breasts. The scent was making him dizzy.

"I'm not green." Steven pulled on the tie. "I hate this thing."

She patted the knot with her long, graceful fingers. "It looks great. Take a deep breath, okay? No passing out during my speech."

Kelsey was valedictorian of their class. Smart on top of gorgeous. She could have had any guy she wanted during high school, except for that chastity vow she'd made to her father. A vow that would end tonight, in Steven's arms, with champagne.

He told himself he wasn't nervous about Kelsey.

He had bigger things to be nervous about.

Eddie nudged his side and showed him a silver flask. "One for the road?"

"You keep it," Steven said.

He pulled on his tie again. It was dumb that everyone had to dress up under their graduation robes. Why couldn't they wear shorts and flip-flops? The only girl in the room not wearing a dress was Robin McGee, the self-appointed radical feminist lesbian of their class, who'd successfully forced the school board to let her wear slacks. She was standing over by the piano with Denny, both of them laughing about something. They were joined by Sean Garrity, the most openly gay teenager Steven knew.

Steven didn't dislike Robin or Sean. They both worked for his mother at her bookstore, as did Denny. But did Denny really have to hang out with them so often? People suspected him of being gay just by association. And Denny was gay, sure, but that was a secret only Steven knew.

People who suspected Denny also suspected Steven, which was totally unfair. And which was maybe why Steven had spent the last two years chasing girls…

In the Secret Yearbook in his head, Steven noted "Most Likely to Overcompensate" beside his own picture.

"Did you hear me?" Kelsey was still standing right in front of him, her perfect eyebrows quirked over her deep blue eyes.

"Huh?"

"I got the key to my dad's boat. We're all set."

He also knew, from her text messages and weekly updates, that she'd also bought condoms and lube, and had stocked up on a morning-after pill in case anything ripped or ended up where it shouldn't be. She was (a) Most Likely to Write a Book on Good Sexual Health, and (b) Most Likely to Teach Teenage Girls How Not To Get Pregnant.

Kelsey asked, "What's wrong?"

"I ate something bad for lunch," he lied.

"Do you want to sit down?" she asked.

Eddie burped in Steven's ear. "Navy SEALs don't need to sit down. They eat nails for breakfast. They parachute out of planes without parachutes. Steven's going to be Admiral SEAL before you know it."

Steven wished Eddie would shut up. He was the only one on Fisher Key who knew the truth. Maybe in some universe, lying to your friends and family and classmates was hilarious. Not in Steven's, though.

Eddie took a quick hit off his flask. "Hey, look who came. Prince Valiant."

The graduating class only had fifty-three students in it. Fifty-four if you counted Brian Vandermark. Brian had no entry in Steven's Secret Yearbook. His family had moved to Fisher Key over Christmas vacation. He'd transferred lots of credit from some rich private school in Boston, and was enrolled in college AP classes online, so hardly ever had to come to school. He had floppy blond hair, wore thick glasses, and had made no friends.

He was standing in the corner now, talking to no one, reading a paperback.

Who brings a book to graduation? What a dork.

Mrs. Harding, their elderly music teacher, clapped her hands together. "All right, now! Line up in alphabetical order. You've done it enough that you know where to stand."

Kelsey kissed Steven on the cheek. "See you soon," she promised, and glided off.

As usual, Steven ended up third in line, right behind Denny. Denny came first alphabetically, but Steven was older by two minutes, which counted as more important. Aaron Adams, skinny and awkward, would lead the procession into the auditorium.

"What if I trip and fall?" Aaron fretted.

Denny said, "You won't trip."

"I fall all the time," Aaron said.

Steven said, "You fall down and I'll step on you."

"He won't step on you," Denny promised. "Because you're not going to trip or fall."

Pomp and Circumstance started up in the auditorium. Steven looked down the line at his classmates. The soccer team guys—Sammy, Enrique, Logan. The smart girls, like Kelsey and Robin. The dorks and the cheerleaders and everyone in between. Most of them had known each other since the first grade. In a few minutes, they'd be graduates, and in a few months they'd be off to different colleges or jobs, and ten years from now they'd hardly be in touch.

Kelsey caught his gaze and smiled broadly at him.

Prince Valiant, all the way at the end of the line, struggled with the zipper on his gown and dropped his book.

Steven turned to Denny. "I'm going to throw up."

"What?"

"Right here, on both of us."

"No, you won't," Denny said, making that sour face he always did when he wanted his own way. He tugged Steven's tie loose. "You just need air."

Mrs. Harding said, "Okay, Aaron, go!" and Aaron started walking.

Denny put his hands on Steven's shoulders. "Just breathe deep and follow me. You'll be fine."

The music grew louder. The next thing he knew, Steven was marching forward and everyone in the auditorium was clapping. The stage lights dazzled him for a moment until his eyes focused on his parents, sitting in the aisle. Dad looked impossibly big in his official police uniform, and Mom, always short beside him, was wearing the green and red dress that reminded him of a tropical bird.

They both looked proud enough to burst. And that was a huge problem. Dad, especially, was going to be damn disappointed when he found out that Steven had gone to Miami to enlist and been turned down by the Navy.

When he found out that Steven and Eddie had faked the enlistment papers that Steven had brandished at the kitchen table.

When he found out that his son was a liar and a fraud.

Steven was never going to be a Navy SEAL.

CHAPTER THREE

Three weeks earlier, Brian Vandermark had agreed to go to his high school graduation only if he could bring his boyfriend to the ceremony.

"What boyfriend?" his mother asked, dropping carrots and celery into the turbo-juice machine on the kitchen counter.

His stepfather, Henrik, didn't look up from his computer tablet. "If it makes you happy, sure."

Brian knew he was lucky. His parents never gave him any grief about being gay. Too many of his friends back home couldn't even tell their families, or had told them only to be interrogated—are you sure, maybe you're wrong, how can you do this to us? But Brian's mom had brought up the subject when he was thirteen, and again before she married Henrik. They loved him for who he was, not his orientation.

"What boyfriend?" his mother asked, adding green apples into the juicer. "You haven't dated anyone since we moved here."

"You can always find a date on the Internet," Henrik said.

"I was thinking about Christopher," Brian said.

Mom turned off the juicer. The blades slowed down as the last juice dribbled out. "Is that a good idea?"

Brian shrugged. "We're still friends. And he'd do it if I asked. Can we pay for his airfare?"

"Sure," Henrik said.

"Only if you're certain," Mom added.

Which is how Brian's ex-boyfriend Christopher Morgan ended up on a direct flight from Boston to Miami, stepping off the plane in tight jeans, an even tighter blue T-shirt, and a garment bag slung over his shoulders. Brian hoped for a kiss, though he worried about what kind—passionate? Chaste? With tongue or without? But there was no kiss. Christopher gave him a big hug instead, followed by a manly slug to the arm.

"Florida boy!" Christopher exclaimed. "Where's your suntan? And what's with the glasses? I know you have contacts."

"They itch," Brian said.

Christopher cocked his head. "You look good anyway."

They retrieved Christopher's suitcase, threw his stuff into the back of Brian's Honda, and headed south with the sunroof open.

"When are you coming back to civilization?" Christopher asked as he typed messages on his phone.

"MIT orientation is the third week of August."

"Still planning to live in the dorms? Your stepdad could buy you a condo."

"I like dorms."

"I'm renting an apartment with Dave and Jay," Christopher said. "In the Back Bay. Three Musketeers."

Once, they'd been the Four Musketeers, but Brian ignored the pang of that.

Christopher laughed at something on his phone and started typing again. "So how are we doing this thing tonight? Do you want me to be draped all over you? Suck face on the dance floor?"

"No!"

"Why not? Don't want to shock the locals?"

Brian tightened his grip on the steering wheel. "I don't care what they think."

"So why not?"

"It wouldn't be…honest."

"One day you're going to get over being the choir boy," Christopher snorted. "I totally want to be there when that happens."

But it wasn't happening tonight, Brian thought morosely just a few hours later. He was standing by the dance floor at the Fisher Key

Yacht Club, just another unhappy wallflower. White lights twinkled overhead, swaying in the breeze from the open patio doors. Couples danced in front of him. Parents and chaperones had clustered over in the main lounge with champagne while the graduates feasted on the buffet and snuck alcohol in from the parking lot.

"Hey!" That was Sean Garrity, the only openly gay teenager in the school. He was skinny and freckled and had spiky hair, but his smile was genuine. "Where've you been keeping him?"

Brian played dumb. "Keeping who?"

"Mr. Handsome Secret, obviously. Who knew you were a member of the club?"

"It's no one's business."

Sean snickered. "On an island, it's everyone's business. The Rainbow Coalition of Fisher Key High could have used your support months ago."

As far as Brian knew, the Rainbow Coalition was maybe four kids, five at most, including Sean and the lesbian who'd sued the school board so she could wear pants to graduation.

"I'm not involved in anything. I'm leaving in August," he said, watching Christopher bump and grind with three girls who'd come without dates.

"Leave Mr. Handsome Secret behind," Sean suggested. "We'll make him feel right at home."

Christopher was doing his part to play dutiful date. Between songs he would swing by to see if Brian wanted anything to drink (no) or wanted to dance (definitely not), and each time, his breath smelled more and more like booze. Brian lingered by the dance floor, hung out on the patio for a while, and wished he'd brought his book along. Finally, he drifted downstairs to the game room, where the Anderson twins were bickering over a game of pool.

"You shoot like a girl."

"You shoot like you're blind."

"I could totally sink that blindfolded."

"I bet you a dollar that you can't."

One of the twins was the smart one and the other was the jock, but Brian couldn't tell them apart. Both of them looked extremely handsome—ties discarded, shirt buttons undone, sleeves rolled up. They had dark hair and brown eyes, with the long, lean bodies of swimmers.

"I'll take that bet."

"You've got a blindfold?"

"Use your tie."

One of the twins lined up the shot, then fastened his tie over his eyes. In the doorway, Brian shifted to get a closer look. The other twin glanced his way.

"Think he can do it?"

Brian blinked. "Maybe."

"I can totally do it," said the blindfolded twin. He picked up the stick and felt carefully for the cue ball.

His brother said, "I didn't say you could touch."

"Didn't say I couldn't." With one swift, sure release, the blindfolded twin knocked the four ball into the corner pocket and ripped off the tie. "Ha!"

The other twin looked bored. "Can't do it again, Steven."

Brian offered, "I can do a jump shot."

They both frowned at him.

"I can," he insisted.

"Let's see it," Steven said.

Under their scrutiny, he lined up the cue ball, blocked it with the six, and then set up the eight farther down the table. Sweat pooled under his armpits. He hoped he didn't look too nervous. Trying to show off was always a bad idea. Especially in front of the two hottest guys in school.

"He's not going to make it," said Steven.

"Bet you a dollar he does."

"You're on."

Brian angled the pool stick and drove it downward. The cue ball jumped exactly as the laws of physics said it should. The eight rolled into the pocket perfectly.

"It's just one trick shot," Steven groused.

Denny smiled at Brian. "He's jealous."

It was the kind of flirty smile that Christopher used to give him. But Brian told himself he had to be wrong, because no way was either of the twins gay. Not unless the Rainbow Coalition at Fisher High was bigger than he'd thought.

"Not jealous," Steven said. "Anyone can get lucky once."

Footsteps thumped down the carpeted stairs outside the game room. Eddie Ibarra burst in, lipstick on his cheek and a bottle of (supposedly) root beer in hand. With him was a pretty girl whose name Brian couldn't remember, even though she'd been valedictorian. Chelsea? Kelsey?

"What are you two doing?" Eddie demanded of the twins. "The party's upstairs."

"And it's time for us to go, Steven," the girl added, tapping her toes.

Steven lined up another shot. "I just need to teach Denny a lesson."

"And Prince Valiant here?" Eddie said, eyeing Brian.

Brian tried not to flinch. For some reason, he ended up collecting nicknames wherever he went—Floppy and Rabbit Ears and once, for a whole year, Schwinn (although the bike accident hadn't been his fault. Not at all.).

"My name's Brian," he said.

"Yeah, Prince Brian," Eddie sneered. "And your prince of a boyfriend. He's not welcome here."

"Shut up, Eddie," Denny said.

"Agreed," Steven said.

But Eddie just took two steps closer to Brian, his chin thrust forward. "Just because you're gay doesn't mean you have to flaunt it like that faggot Sean Garrity."

Denny stepped in between Eddie and Brian. "Nobody wants to hear that redneck trailer-trash talk—"

Eddie swung a punch at him. Denny caught it, twisted Eddie's right arm up behind his back, and slammed him down on the pool table. Brian winced at the solid thump of it.

"Let me go!" Eddie raged.

Denny shook his head. "Not until you promise to play nice."

"Fuck you! Faggots! You and Garrity and Prince Valiant—"

Denny twisted his arm tighter. Eddie yelped.

"You shouldn't make him mad," Steven said calmly.

"You want to drive around all summer with your arm in a cast, or do you want to think about what you're saying?" Denny asked.

Eddie grunted but said nothing. Kelsey's gaze flicked between the two brothers. Brian kept his own face blank. He didn't like violence, but he didn't like Eddie either.

Steven scooped up two balls and lined them up near Eddie's head. He picked up his stick and drawled, "You're blocking my shot."

"Asstard," Denny said, although it wasn't clear who he was talking to. He let Eddie go and stepped back. Eddie reared to his feet, his face red and drool at the corner of his mouth.

"Sissies, all of you," he spat out, and stalked out of the room.

Brian's mouth was dry. "You didn't have to do that for me."

Denny said, "I didn't do it for you."

"No, you did it because you could." Steven didn't sound mad about it, but he didn't sound happy either. Brian wondered if he and Eddie were friends. Steven knocked the nine ball into a pocket. "He's going to be pissed tomorrow."

Denny replied, "He's pissed now. Do I look worried?"

Kelsey said, "Can we go now?"

"Yeah." Steven tossed his stick to Denny. "Don't wait up."

They left. Upstairs, the music shifted from fast and heavy to soft and romantic. Brian was abruptly aware of being alone in a room with the insanely hot guy who'd just defended his honor, or something like that. The air seemed warm and scarce, as if it didn't have enough oxygen for both of them.

"Why'd you come tonight?" Denny asked. "You could have just stayed home and collected your diploma by mail."

Brian took his time answering. "I guess because you only get to graduate once."

"And why'd you bring your boyfriend?"

That was easier. "I didn't want to hide who I am."

"Or you wanted to show it off."

Brian squared his shoulders. "Maybe."

Denny's expression was inscrutable. "Okay."

He left the game room. Brian followed him upstairs. A few couples still lingered on the dance floor or by the buffet, but mostly everyone else had cleared out for other parties or private get-togethers. Brian couldn't see Christopher anywhere. That wasn't much of a surprise, but it stung anyway.

"Come on, Denny!" a girl called out. "We're going to Jennifer's!"

"Best party on the island tonight," Denny said casually. "You going?"

Brian wasn't much for parties—too many strangers, too much noise. At the same time, the idea of spending more time with Denny was very tempting.

"I wasn't invited," Brian said.

"You don't need an invitation."

"I have to find my friend."

"Call him," Denny said.

Brian tried Christopher's number, but it went straight to voice mail.

"Come on," Denny cajoled him. "It's a small island. Send him the address. You'll have a good time."

Part of Brian told him to be loyal and stick around until Christopher returned. The other part, much louder, told him to seize the day. Graduation night only came once, after all.

"Okay, sure," Brian said. "I'll follow you over in my car."

Denny smiled that handsome smile again. "Forget cars. I know a shortcut."

CHAPTER FOUR

The boat that belonged to Kelsey's father was a vintage cabin cruiser with a small but well-designed galley. Steven pulled green grapes, Swiss cheese, some turkey slices, and an apple from the refrigerator, silently thanking whoever had stocked it. Sex always left him famished, ready to restock at an all-you-can-eat buffet.

"Steven?" Kelsey called out. "Did you knock me up and run away? That would be terrible."

He finished piling the food on a plate and went to the aft cabin. Kelsey was stretched out on the narrow bunk, covered with a white sheet. She didn't look lonely. She looked like she was messaging someone on her phone. Beside her, the open porthole let in the smells and sounds of the Atlantic.

"Don't even joke about getting pregnant."

She smiled widely at him. "Just checking."

"Who are you talking to?"

"Jennifer. Big party at her house, right now."

Steven perched on the edge of the bunk and ate the apple while Kelsey kept typing. Kelsey and Jennifer O'Malley were best friends. He liked Jen, and he liked her big house overlooking the water. He bet the party would go on all night.

"Tell her I was totally worth waiting for," he suggested.

"You want us to compare notes?"

"No," he said. That didn't sound like a good idea at all. He'd been with Jennifer only twice, when they were sixteen.

Kelsey put her phone away. She propped herself up on one elbow, took a grape, and popped it into her mouth. "I would tell her that you were fantastic. Kind of fast."

About to bite down on a wedge of cheese, Steven paused. "Fast?"

"And fantastic."

"But you said fast."

Kelsey shrugged. "Like you were maybe rushing things."

His face grew hot. "I wasn't rushing anything."

"Or maybe I was." She popped another grape into her mouth. "We need to do it again, more slowly."

He certainly could do it again, but no one had ever criticized him before. Not in bed, anyway. Especially not someone who'd never done it before, so how could she tell?

"Anything else I should do differently?" he asked sarcastically.

She stroked the side of his face. "Don't be insulted. It's a good thing when someone gives you feedback. That's how you get better."

"Maybe I'm just fine right now."

"You are," she agreed. "I said 'fantastic.' But slow is good, too. Don't you want to practice?"

The sheet was slipping off her shoulder. In another minute or two it would fall completely. Steven put the food aside, kissed her on the mouth, and then kissed her neck. Her skin tasted like baby oil. She made a little happy noise.

"We can practice all summer long," she murmured. "I got a book to use."

Steven pulled back. "A book?"

"The *Kama Sutra*. It's an ancient Indian guide."

"I know what it is," Steven lied. "Maybe I just like it American style."

Kelsey frowned at him. "You need to have an open mind. I'm moving to Miami in September, and you're going to be in the military."

He didn't correct her about that.

She added, "Don't you want to be as good at this as you can be?"

"Maybe I'm good right now!"

"You're okay," Kelsey said quietly. "I knew that already. All your ex-girlfriends said so."

Steven sat back so quickly that he hit his head on the bulkhead. The crack of it made his eyes water.

Kelsey cupped his chin. "Are you okay?"

"No," he complained. "You broke me."

She kissed him lightly on the lips "Well, fix yourself. We've got some practicing to do."

❖

"How is this a shortcut?" Brian asked as Denny steered a small white motorboat away from the twinkling lights of the yacht club.

"We're avoiding gridlock," Denny replied.

Gridlock on Fisher Key meant three cars at the only traffic light in town. Not that Brian was going to complain. A warm summer night, a half-moon in the sky, and a handsome guy at the helm? Graduation night was turning out a lot better than he'd imagined.

"What if we tip over? I'm not the best swimmer around," Brian said.

"I'll save you."

"That's comforting." Brian gripped the edge of his seat tighter. "Technically, are we stealing this boat?"

"Technically, we're borrowing. It's Sean's dad's, but he lets me use it."

"Why?"

"Steven and I helped him out once. One of his employees was stealing from his company, and we caught him." Denny said it casually, as if teenagers solved crimes every day. "I have my own boat, but it's at my house."

"You own a boat?"

"Sure."

Brian wondered what his life would have been like if he'd grown up on Fisher Key. Boats, tides, and deep-sea fishing, instead of cold winters and city traffic. He'd never have met Christopher and had his heart broken.

He snuck a sideways look at Denny. Didn't he know what rumors would start if they arrived at the party together?

Maybe Denny was thinking the same thing, because he looked out at the horizon and said, "I'm not gay, you know. That was just Eddie being a jerk."

Brian had been telling himself not to get his hopes up. Insanely hot, smart, and gay? The trifecta. And he wasn't going to win it tonight.

He tried not to look disappointed. Instead, he asked, "So why did you invite me out here?"

"Because it sucks to get ditched at your own graduation party."

The chugging motor was the only sound for a few moments. Brian watched the shoreline, looking for his parents' house. He'd never seen it from the water.

"They say you're going into the Coast Guard Academy," he said.

"I go away for training next month. They call it 'Swab Summer.'"

"Why the Coast Guard? Why not the Navy?"

Denny said, "The Navy fights wars. The Coast Guard rescues people. How about you?"

"I'm going to MIT."

"Yeah?" Denny looked impressed. "Science geek?"

"No. I'm going to study history."

"They have that there?"

"Sure. They have lots of things."

"Was that what you were reading before graduation? I saw you brought a book to the band room," Denny said.

Brian didn't tell him he'd brought the book because he was too shy to talk to anyone there. "Biography of Marie Antoinette. She got married to the future king of France when she was only fourteen. Isn't that crazy?"

As soon as the words were out of his mouth, he regretted them. Eighteenth-century history wasn't usually a popular topic in teen circles. Denny was going to think he was a total idiot.

But Denny didn't seem to be listening. He was staring at a silhouette on the water nearby. He cut the motor.

"Look at her," he said. "Isn't she beautiful?"

The boat ahead of them was long and low in the waves, her sails down for the night. Brian didn't know much about boats, and it was too dark to make out many details, but Denny certainly looked happy.

"Whose is it?" Brian asked.

"I don't know," Denny said. "Steven and I saw her out on the water today. I'd give anything for a boat like that."

The motorboat rocked gently beneath them, water lapping at the hull. Brian took in a deep breath of salty air. The brass fittings on the yacht gleamed in the moonlight. Perfect. Denny's expression was open and reverential, like a kid at Christmas.

Maybe one day someone would look at Brian that way.

The breeze shifted, salt giving way to the acrid smell of smoke.

"What is that?" Brian asked.

Red flames erupted from the yacht's foredeck.

Denny stood up, his reverence turning to horror. "She's on fire!"

CHAPTER FIVE

Denny brought the motorboat closer to the burning yacht, yelling, "Hey! Fire!"

No one answered. No sign of life anywhere on *The Tempest*, but someone might be unconscious or trapped below deck. Denny handed his cell phone to Brian and kicked off his shoes.

"Call for help," he said. "Tell them we're off Beacon Point."

"Where are you going?"

Denny dove off into the warm salty water. He surfaced a few yards later and swam with sure strokes to the yacht's starboard side. The fire was licking up her bow toward the masts with frightening speed. She had been built to be close to the water and he had no trouble grabbing her lines.

Just as he started to haul himself upward, an enormous whoosh blasted from deep within the ship. A bellow of hot air pushed him backward into the deep.

Explosion, Denny thought, and then he thought no more.

The blast from *The Tempest* made Brian throw up his arms and stagger backward over the side of the motorboat and into the ocean. He hit hard, water slamming up his nose and mouth. The crash took his glasses away instantly. He choked, flailed, tried to break through to the surface. The only thing around him was blackness, and he was drowning.

I'm too young to drown, he thought in dismay.

Panic made him kick his legs wildly. He reached out, felt something like the wind on his hand. He moved in that direction. Broke into the fresh air, coughing so hard he thought his eyes were popping out of his head.

He couldn't see anything, couldn't breathe right, couldn't find anything to hold on to.

And he didn't know where Denny was. Was he drowning just a few feet away, injured and helpless?

Brian hacked out more water. His vision was full of hot red stars that had nothing to do with the sky. He could smell burning wood and fuel, and there was a fuzzy red and yellow ball of flame nearby. But where was the damn motorboat? Where was Denny?

His shoes were dragging him down, and his limbs felt uncoordinated. He tried not to panic again, but the water was closing over his head again—

"Easy!" a man's voice said, close to his ear. "Hold on, kid."

Strong, confident arms wrapped around his chest. Brian was so startled he sucked in more water and started to struggle. His rescuer didn't let him go.

"My friend," Brian coughed out.

"What friend?"

"He's here somewhere!"

A moment later, Brian felt his hands being guided to something hard and high—the motorboat. Smoke and ash blew into his face.

"Stay here," the man said and dove away.

Brian started to pull himself into the boat. It was ridiculously hard because the stupid thing kept trying to slide out from under his rubbery hands. When he did succeed, he collapsed half on and half off a bench, still coughing.

The yacht was still aflame, the mystery guy had disappeared, and where was Denny?

With a splash and a gasp, the stranger broke the surface. Denny was in his arms, limp and unmoving.

"Here, take him!"

Brian leaned over the side and helped haul Denny aboard.

"Don't die," Brian begged him. "Breathe, don't die."

The stranger pulled himself in. He was tall and well-built in the red light of the burning boat. He was clad only in tight black swim trunks.

"He's not going to die," the man said, and gave Denny what Brian thought was the Heimlich maneuver.

Immediately Denny began to vomit up water. He flailed in the stranger's arms until he could bend over and choke out more. Brian held Denny's shoulder, steadying him.

"You kids nearly got yourself killed," the stranger said.

"Where did you come from?" Brian asked.

"I was swimming by," was the answer, and it didn't sound like the stranger was joking.

Before Brian could ask more, the man started up the motor and steered them away from the burning wreck. A Coast Guard boat with spinning red lights was rounding Beacon Point, and other boats had started out from land.

Denny continued to cough and wheeze, but he didn't seem hurt.

Somehow Brian didn't think they were going to make it to Jennifer O'Malley's party.

Steven heard the boom of an explosion and looked out the porthole to see *The Tempest* on fire several hundred yards offshore. The fuel tank must have exploded. He abandoned what he'd been doing to Kelsey and reached for his pants.

"Where are you going?" Kelsey asked breathlessly.

"Someone's in trouble!"

He raced along the dock barefoot, shoes and shirt in hand. The explosion had brought several spectators down from the yacht club, including Steven's parents and the club president, Ed Berman.

"I hope no one was aboard," Mom said, her gaze worried.

"We'd better go see," Ed Berman said. "We'll take my boat."

"Can I come too, Dad?" Steven asked.

His father disconnected the cell phone he'd been using to call the police station. Although off duty, he was still in uniform—the biggest guy on the island, an ex-football star from the University of Miami. He eyed Steven's disheveled clothes and said, "Looks like you're busy enough."

Mom agreed, "Yes, you should stay here."

"I won't get in the way," Steven said. "You might need a hand."

Ed Berman had volunteered his boat, but he wasn't quite sober enough to steer. Dad took the helm and Steven got to tag along after all. Four minutes out, they met up with Sean Garrity's motorboat.

"Dennis?" Dad asked, and Steven's jaw dropped. The boat was full with his twin, Brian Vandermark, and the guy with the fishing boat they'd met out on the water that afternoon.

All of them were drenched and Denny was coughing like he'd swallowed half the ocean.

Dad's face creased with concern. "What are you doing out here, Dennis?"

"Boat blew up, Dad," was Denny's answer.

"I can see that," Dad huffed out.

Once aboard Ed Berman's cruiser, Dad checked both Denny and Brian for injuries and Steven got them blankets from below deck. The man from the fishing boat said his name was Nathan Carter.

"I'm training for a triathlon," he said. "Saw the explosion and found these kids in the water."

"I'm glad you did," Dad said. "You a Navy man?"

Nathan Carter paused. "Was. Not any longer."

He looked exactly like the kind of super-athlete who thought nothing of swimming around the Atlantic Ocean late at night. But up close, Steven could see a long scar down the back of Carter's leg. Maybe he'd gotten out of the military on a disability. Or maybe he wasn't what he said he was. It seemed awfully coincidental that he'd been out there just in time to save Denny and Brian.

Dad turned to Denny. "And what were you two doing out here?"

Which led to a jumbled story about going to Jennifer O'Malley's party via boat, and Brian needed a ride, and no, Denny hadn't been drinking, swear it.

Steven watched Dad carefully for signs of doubt. Did he suspect that Denny and Brian had been on the water for some romantic reason? Could he tell Denny was gay? Their parents occasionally hinted that Denny should date more, and he had in fact taken a girl to the prom, but that was only a friendship thing.

"And then we stopped because it's a beautiful ship." Denny gazed sorrowfully at the still-burning wreck. "Was beautiful."

"Damn shame," Ed Berman said from the helm. "Hell of an accident."

"If it was an accident," Carter said.

Steven asked, "You think it was deliberate?"

"I saw someone swimming away from the boat just before it blew." Carter's voice and face were both grim. "You better ask him."

Chapter Six

Brian's parents seriously freaked out over the almost-getting-killed part.

"This is supposed to be a nice peaceful island!" Henrik ranted, stalking around their living room in a big circle. "Peaceful does not mean things blowing up!"

His Danish accent was getting thicker. Half the time, Brian forgot that Henrik came from overseas, but the accent always appeared when he was upset. Brian decided that now was not a good time to disagree. The Florida Keys had never been particularly peaceful. Not with drunk drivers careening down the Overseas Highway, drug runners zooming offshore, even the occasional murder or two.

Mom petted Brian's knee. "Accidents happen. We were lucky."

Brian nodded dumbly. Maybe he was in shock. He didn't feel like he was in shock. Mostly, he felt cold. The air-conditioning was set too high, as usual. He was glad for the green blanket Mom had wrapped him in. The blanket also kept him from getting the sofa wet. It was a nice sofa, white leather to match the white rug and white walls and white curtains.

The darkest things in the room were the glass doors overlooking the Florida Straits, the half moon still visible in the sky. Well, kind of visible. Blurry visible. He wondered where his spare eyeglasses were.

Henrik tugged at his thinning hair and continued stalking around the room. "Let's see what the FBI says. Accident or maybe not an accident. Smugglers. Spies. Who knows? Murder on *The Temper!*"

"*Tempest*," Mom corrected him.

Henrik's face turned redder.

"Come on, honey," Mom said. "You'll feel better after a hot shower."

Under the hot spray of water, Brian remembered the feel of Denny's shoulder under his hand. The way Denny had ridden close to him on the way back to shore. Not that it meant anything, because Denny had said he wasn't gay. Wasn't gay at all. Was entirely heterosexual.

Actually, Denny hadn't said that last part at all.

He crawled into his comfortable bed, glad to be away from anything that rocked or bobbed back and forth. He was asleep in seconds. In his dreams, *The Tempest* whooshed into crimson flames over and over again, and Denny was a dark body floating lifelessly in the water. He struggled awake to hear voices in the kitchen.

"—totally in flames, man!" Christopher was saying, loud and excited. "It's the first time I ever saw something blow up in real life!"

Brian's mom said something, her voice pitched low.

"Oh, sorry! I'll keep my voice down. Do you have any nachos?"

Brian pulled a pillow over his head and went back to sleep. The next thing he knew, sunlight was streaming through his bedroom windows. When he went out into the kitchen his mother was assembling a gift basket of fresh fruit, homemade granola, and dark chocolate from Belgium, along with fresh cut leaves for decoration and a large blue ribbon to top everything off.

"Who's that for?" Brian asked.

"Nathan Carter, for saving your life," Mom said. "I want you to take it over to him."

"Me?" he squeaked out.

"He saved your life."

"He saved Denny's life. I was doing fine."

"It's the least we can do."

Henrik was sipping from his enormous coffee mug. "I could write him a check."

"No!" Brian said. "That's not what you do. It's not like a reward for finding a stray dog."

Both of them looked at him with concern.

"Are you feeling all right?" Mom asked.

"I'm fine. "

"I made an appointment with Dr. Elliot," she said. "Just in case. Go get dressed, I'll run you over."

"Mom, I don't need a doctor."

"Just a quick appointment. You always want to make sure about these things."

They stopped by the public marina on the way. Carter was on the deck of the most dilapidated boat that Brian had ever seen on the water. Now that he was wearing his glasses again and it was daylight, Brian could see he was incredibly handsome. Drop-dead handsome, like a hunky calendar model.

"Ahoy!" Mom said. "Anchors aweigh!"

Thus commenced several embarrassing minutes while Mom thanked Carter over and over. Carter looked surprised by the gift basket, but nodded politely.

"I'm glad I was useful," was all he said about saving Denny and Brian.

Dr. Elliot's waiting room was empty when they got to his office on the highway. The doctor smelled like cigarettes, but he was friendly and efficient as he examined Brian's ears and pupils.

"You were right there when that boat blew up, hmm?" Elliot asked. "Must have been impressive."

"If you like things blowing up," Brian said.

Elliot picked up his stethoscope. "Things are always blowing up around those Anderson boys. Breathe deeply for me and hold it."

When he could talk again, Brian asked, "What kinds of things?"

"Hmmm?"

"Are always blowing up around the Andersons?"

"They lead very eventful lives. Boy detectives, don't you know. Always helping out their dad and anyone else who needs something solved or fixed."

The doctor couldn't find anything wrong with him, so he sent Brian off with recommendations for rest and aspirin. Mom drove him home with her wedding ring tapping restlessly on the steering wheel. When they got home Christopher was gone, off retrieving Brian's car from the yacht club.

"I told him that would help redeem himself," Henrik said from the kitchen island, where he was pouring himself coffee.

"Redeem himself from what?" Brian asked.

Mom said, "He was high when he came home last night."

"Oh." Brian eased himself onto a stool. "Sorry."

"You're not the one who broke the law," Henrik replied. "What if he had been caught and arrested? More problems. His parents would blame us."

Actually, Christopher's parents were just as likely to smoke their own pot, but Brian didn't think he should point that out. Henrik was very strict about drugs and speed limits and rules. Maybe it was that discipline that had made him a millionaire businessman. Brian didn't know much about Henrik's business, but he certainly had a lot of money.

Mom sat on the stool beside Brian. "We don't think you and Christopher should go down to Key West tonight."

"What?" Brian asked. "Why not?"

"You need rest," Mom said.

"And the police might need to talk to you some more," Henrik said.

"I told Captain Anderson everything I know," Brian said. "I'm not going to suddenly remember some important fact or something. Besides, I can rest down there with him just like I can rest here. And I promised Christopher."

The promise had been a weekend at a very nice hotel overlooking the ocean. Two beds, just so Christopher wouldn't feel pressured to rekindle anything—but hey, if things happened, they happened, and when he'd made the reservations Brian secretly hoped they would.

Henrik stared down in his coffee cup. "It's not a good time to go. Some reporters have called for interviews, and who knows what else might happen. Your mother and I—well, we worry."

Mom squeezed Brian's hand. "Can't you stay?"

"It's the day after I graduated from high school, and Christopher goes back to Boston on Monday," Brian said. "I've done everything you ever asked me to do, including leave all my friends to come down here to the middle of nowhere. So if I want to take Christopher to Key West, just like I promised him, I think you need to let me."

Mom and Henrik looked at each other.

"We worry," Mom said.

Brian felt curiously like he was the parent and they were the children. "Nothing bad is going to happen. I promise."

CHAPTER SEVEN

"Wake up, Dennis Andrew," said a familiar voice.

Denny cracked open his eyes and gave Steven the stink-eye. "Go away."

"You going to just sleep all day?" Fresh from his morning run, Steven peeled off his damp T-shirt and threw it on Denny's chest. "Enjoy your celebrity status while you can. I've got thirty-two text messages on my phone because of you. *Apparently* your phone is on the bottom of the ocean, goofball."

Denny pushed the disgusting T-shirt off him and closed his eyes again. For years he'd begged for his own bedroom. He'd offered to build an addition himself, or erect a tree house, or put an RV in the yard. Because it was a special kind of torture to spend eighteen years in a cramped room with someone who wouldn't even let you sleep in the morning after you'd nearly gotten killed.

Steven dropped to the floor and started doing SEAL-style push-ups. "Seriously. If you don't get up and prove to Mom and Dad that you're okay, they'll drag you to the hospital."

"I'll be up in an hour."

"Now, if you want to find out more about Nathan Carter."

For a moment, Denny's mind was blank. Nathan who? Oh. The Greek god. Denny remembered only fragments of the explosion—a burst of heat, floating, hacking up half the ocean. Nathan Carter had saved him. Nathan Carter had pulled him out of the ocean and maybe even given him mouth-to-mouth resuscitation.

"I'm taking a shower," Denny said, pushing out of bed.

"Me first!" Steven protested.

"Nope." Denny shut the door first. The shower was the only place in the whole house where he could get privacy.

Thinking of Nathan Carter's sleek body and handsome face meant Denny needed privacy right now. Desperately.

Halfway through the shower he remembered Brian Vandermark, too—Brian without his glasses, his wet shirt clinging to him. Brian's shy smile and floppy hair and the way he'd watched his boyfriend dance with other people.

"Hey!" Steven pounded on the bathroom door. "Hurry up!"

Denny finished up ten minutes later, turned the bathroom over to Steven, and got dressed. He found his parents in the small kitchen. Dad was already in his uniform, sitting at the table with a cup of coffee and a pile of computer printouts. Mom was still wearing her nightgown and was peering inside the refrigerator in despair.

"How do you feel, kiddo?" Dad asked, giving Denny a close look.

"I'm okay," Denny said. He kissed his mother and reached past her for the egg tray. "How about some omelets?"

Mom smiled. "I was hoping someone would say that."

She didn't cook. Dad didn't cook either. Well, not unless you counted microwave food and noodles. It was a miracle that Denny and Steven had survived childhood long enough to learn to use the stove. "Any news on *The Tempest,* Dad?"

"Lots of interesting stuff," Dad said. "She's some kind of classic, all right. Built in 1932 for a steel magnate. Won all sorts of awards. Sold a dozen times, had a bunch of different names. Last reported stolen from a marina in France four years ago."

The phone rang and Mom answered. As owner of the only bookstore on the Middle Keys, she was also president of the Chamber of Commerce and an aid society for Cuban refugees. She'd been born in Havana, a place Denny had seen only in old history books.

He thought of Brian and his love of history. The Florida Keys had a lot of great stories and folklore. Maybe he could get Brian a book about it. A sort of "Sorry I nearly got you killed" gift.

"Yes?" Mom asked, turning away. "Oh, hi. Yes. We didn't get to talk much last night."

Denny stirred the eggs and milk together, then seasoned them with salt and pepper. He asked his father, "What about Nathan Carter?"

"Honorable discharge from the Navy last year. Not sure why." Dad shifted through his papers. "No current job, but he spent the winter down in Key West. He said last night he was training for a triathlon, but there's no record he's ever competed for one before."

Steven came out of the bathroom rubbing a towel over his head. "You said he was a SEAL, Dad."

Dad shifted through the papers again. "Yes."

"So maybe he's just used to swimming around the ocean at night," Denny said.

"Yeah, but it's a big coincidence," Steven said. "Him being there just as it's going up in flames."

"He might be saying the same thing about me," Denny said.

They explained to their father about meeting Carter out on the water, just as *The Tempest* was arriving.

"Hmmm," Dad said. "You think he used his demolitions experience to blow it up?"

"If he was going to blow it up, he wouldn't stick around to save us," Denny said. "Better to have no witnesses at all."

Steven sat down across from Dad. "He said he saw someone else swimming away. Whoever brought *The Tempest* into the harbor, maybe."

"No one knows who that is," Dad said.

Denny poured the omelets onto the hot griddle. "Which way was the swimmer going?"

Dad said, "Toward Beacon Point. But the Coast Guard went over there and didn't find anything."

Mom hung up the phone. "That was Hannah Vandermark. Nice lady. She wanted to see how you were doing, Denny."

"How's Brian?" Denny asked.

"Still sleeping. He's not used to that much excitement." Mom leaned over the cooking omelets. "Yum. Cheese?"

"Coming right up," Denny said.

After breakfast, Dad went off to the station and Mom got ready to open the bookstore at ten. Denny worked there as well, but today was his day off. Which was good, because he needed to go buy a new cell phone.

"And maybe we could swing by and talk to Nathan Carter," he said to Steven.

"You read my mind," Steven replied.

They biked over to the city marina. The first thing Denny saw was *The Tempest*, which had been towed in by the Coast Guard. Yellow tape kept her cordoned off from a few gawkers. With her masts gone and deck in pieces, she was a sad, burnt shell of former glory. All that fine workmanship, destroyed. Denny wanted to weep.

"Awful, awful shame," said Nellie Hill, who was as much a fixture at the marina as the store, the fuel pumps, and the pelicans. In her younger days, she and her husband had sailed around the entire world. She was sitting in her folding chair near the main fence, a straw hat protecting her from the sun. "The things people blow up these days. It's a tragedy."

"Do you know that boat, Miss Nellie?" Steven asked.

"Wish I did," Miss Nellie replied, sipping from her iced coffee. "Wish I'd owned it. No one would go blowing up a boat like that if I had my say."

Denny scanned the docks for Nathan Carter's crappy fishing boat. Miss Nellie said, "Looking for that navy man, are you? He's a good looking one."

"I didn't notice," Denny said.

Steven said, "Have you met him?"

"Nope. So don't go asking me for gossip yet." She laughed. "Give me a day or two, Steven."

They went down to *The Tempest*. Dad had stationed Deputy Lyle Horne to keep people outside the tape. Lyle's uniform was sweat-stained already, and too tight over the belly. He'd gone to Fisher Key High and then the police academy, but everyone knew he was a lousy cop.

A lousy cop with an uncle who happened to be lieutenant governor.

"Heard you nearly got yourself blown up, Denny," Lyle said. "You and some pansy boy."

"I heard you stayed home and read porn all night," Denny said. "Still surfing for underage girls?"

Lyle's face hardened. "You watch your tone, boy."

"It wasn't porn; it was slash fanfic," Steven said.

"Get out of here before I knock both of you into the water," Lyle threatened.

Denny didn't believe the threat, but *The Tempest* was too depressing to look at anymore. He and Steven went over to the *Idle*, but Nathan Carter was either sleeping or out. They biked over to the Overseas Highway, where the road was lined with gas stations, cheap motels, marine stores, and old diners. At Sal's Gas & Go, Denny looked over the cell phones while Steven eyed ceramic conch shells and cheap T-shirts.

"Lost another one, hmm?" Sal sympathized. "Boys like you should buy stock in cell phone companies."

"It wasn't my fault," Denny said.

"It's never your fault," Steven said. His own phone kept buzzing with messages. He checked some and said, "Jennifer O'Malley wants to know if you're dead or alive."

"How touching."

"Eddie says he's sorry for being a jerk."

"Tell him he's an alcoholic lush," Denny said.

He'd forgotten about the fight in the game room, but now he was irritated all over again. Eddie knew better than to say crap about Sean Garrity. He definitely knew better than to make accusations about Denny.

Denny got his new phone and shoved it into his backpack. He'd have to charge it at home. As they biked along the asphalt of the highway Steven checked his phone again. "Kelsey wants me to come over."

"So go."

"She'll just want to have sex."

"Too much information."

"She wants to use an Indian book. The Kim Satre or something."

"And still the information keeps coming," Denny said. "You don't know what the *Kama Sutra* is?"

Steven looked annoyed. "Should I?"

"It's a famous book about sexual positions," Denny said. "She must be pretty adventurous."

He would have said more, just to irritate Steven, but instead stopped at the sight of a news van from Miami. It was parked in the crushed seashell lot next to the Li'l Conch Cafe, which served the best pizza on the island.

"What?" Steven asked.

"News crew," Denny said. "I don't want to talk to them."

"Then we won't."

Denny focused on the car beside the van. "I think that's Brian's car."

"How can you tell?"

"It's got stickers from Fisher Key High and MIT on it. I hope he's not getting pestered."

They circled around to the back dock, which overlooked an inlet and marsh leading to the Gulf of Mexico. Standing by the railing was the guy Brian had brought to the graduation party. Christopher someone. He was posing dramatically for the camera.

"—we saw it explode and were worried, you know, that someone from school was on it," he said. As if he even went to Fisher Key High. "Graduation night, right? It could have been this big tragedy."

The reporter beside him was Janet Hogan from Channel 7 news. She was taller than she appeared on television, with tightly coiled dark hair and coral-red lipstick. Mom hated Janet Hogan because she was anti-Cuban.

"No one was injured, right?" Janet Hogan asked now.

"My friend Brian was nearly killed," Christopher said. "He was on the water. Got nearly blown out of it. He could have drowned."

Denny took a half-step forward. Steven snagged his arm and said, "Ignore him."

"He wasn't even there," Denny fumed.

"So he's exaggerating. Who cares?"

The back door to the cafe opened. Louanne Garrity, Sean's cousin, came out carrying a tray of sodas and French fries, oblivious to the news crew.

"Hey there, Denny, Steven," she said, her red ponytail swinging behind her. "Crazy about that boat last night, huh? I heard one of you nearly got killed!"

Janet Hogan swung their way, her microphone poised for action.

CHAPTER EIGHT

S o how about it, boys?" Janet Hogan asked. "Spill it."
"*No hablo inglés,*" Denny said.
"Ditto," Steven said.

Janet folded her arms. "Don't be coy. After all I've done for you and your father?"

"You nearly ruined the Harper case," Denny told her.

Steven snagged a French fry off of Louanne's tray. "And blew our cover when we were trying to solve the Richardson murder."

"Freedom of the press," Janet Hogan said sharply. "Now, don't you want to catch whoever it is that blew up that lovely boat?"

"Sure," Steven said. "All we have to do is find out who stole it."

She looked intrigued. "Who said it was stolen?"

"Police sources," Steven said.

"When?"

"Not exactly sure," Denny said, which was true. "But I bet a sharp investigative reporter like yourself could find out."

Janet Hogan stalked off on her black high heels to track down the lead. Denny turned to Christopher and said, "What are you doing, going on TV and talking about stuff you don't know about?"

"Who says I don't know?" Christopher protested. "I was there. Watching from the boat ramp at Beacon Point."

Steven and Denny exchanged glances.

"Did you see anyone in the water?" Steven asked.

"What, swimming around? No."

Denny said, "What were you doing on the boat ramp?"

"What do you care?"

"Because our dad's a cop," Steven said. "We help him out. If you know something about a crime and don't come forward, that's obstruction of justice."

Christopher scowled. "We weren't committing any crimes! A little drinking, so what? Nothing happened."

Steven said nothing. Denny scrutinized the light sheen of sweat on Christopher's face, and the way he'd gone pale. Behind Christopher, some white egrets pecked at food in the marsh and the breeze pushed tall grass back and forth. Louanne delivered her food to a couple of tourists at the corner table and watched them all from the corner of her eye.

"I think you're lying," Denny told Christopher.

"Okay, fine," he said. "A little drinking, and we smoked some pot. This girl Lisa found a duffel bag, but there was nothing in it. Some clothes and shoes. Maybe a set of keys. Some homeless guy's stuff. We threw it in the water."

The only Lisa that Denny knew was Lisa Horne, Lyle's younger sister. Nasty girl, and she smoked more than anyone Denny knew. She was also Eddie Ibarra's on-again, off-again girlfriend.

Steven said, "Who else was there?"

"I didn't catch everyone's name," Christopher said sullenly. "Look, are we done? I want to go check on Brian."

He said it as if he cared. But if he'd cared, Denny thought, he would never have been at Beacon Point in the first place.

"The police will be in touch," Steven said solemnly, and they left him there on the patio, scowling at the marsh.

❖

The boat ramp at Beacon Point was at the end of a road branching from the Overseas Highway. They biked out there and searched for the duffel bag Christopher said they'd thrown into the water. The shoreline was all coral and wild mangroves, too rough to search on foot.

"We'll have to come back with the boat," Steven said.

The sun was high and hot by the time they got home. Steven made them both some BLT sandwiches. Denny was looking wiped out. Nearly getting killed could do that to a guy.

"Take a nap," Steven told him. "I'll try to find Lisa Horne."

For once, Denny didn't argue. He stretched out on their lumpy sofa and was asleep within minutes. Steven messaged Eddie but got no response. He called the Horne family at home.

"Steven Anderson! Hello!" That was old Mrs. Horne, the grandmother who always drove around the island in her vintage Cadillac at a speed only slightly faster than a snail. "I haven't seen you in the sports pages this week."

"The season's over, ma'am," Steven said. "I graduated last night."

"Congratulations! Are you the twin going into the Coast Guard or the twin going into the Navy?"

"The Navy, ma'am," he lied. "Is Lisa around? I wanted to talk to her."

"She went shopping," Mrs. Horne said. "I should have such energy. Out all night with friends, and then she and Eddie just left for Miami. Shopping trip. Did you hear about that boat that blew up?"

"Yes, ma'am."

"Investigating the crime, are you?"

"Trying to," Steven admitted.

When he hung up he saw that Kelsey had texted him again, saying "Come on by," and he figured he couldn't keep ignoring her. He took his truck, a fifteen-year-old beater Ford pickup that he'd put a lot of time and money into. Other kids laughed at it, maybe, but they had parents who could afford to buy them cars.

"Most Likely to Be Spoiled Rotten," was how he thought of them—kids who'd never had to earn anything the hard way. The Keys were full of them.

Kelsey's father owned a three-bedroom glass-and-wood home on the Gulf side of the island. His Volvo was in the carport, a bad sign. Steven didn't like seeing fathers the day after he'd slept with their daughters. He was sure they could see it on his face and would be reaching for their shotguns.

"Hey, there," Kelsey said, meeting him at the door. She was wearing a white tank top and pink shorts, her hair pulled back with pink headband. She gave him a quick kiss. "How's your brother?"

"Sleeping," Steven said.

Mr. Carlson came out of his office, a copy of *The New York Times* in hand. He was wearing a crisp white shirt with silver cufflinks and a black striped tie. The house was just as formal, with a lot of framed pictures of Manhattan and Paris. As far as Steven knew, Mr. Carlson had never been outside of Florida.

"Hello, Steven. How was the party last night? I'm sorry I had to miss it."

"A boat blew up, Daddy," Kelsey said.

"Really?" Mr. Carlson looked intrigued. "On purpose?"

Steven said, "Not by accident."

"Do you know who owned it? He might need a lawyer."

"Daddy," Kelsey complained.

Mr. Carlson grinned. Legal jokes. "Are you looking forward to boot camp, Steven?"

"Yes, sir. Every day."

Kelsey pulled Steven down the hall to her blue-and-white bedroom decorated with school pictures and teddy bears.

"Door open!" Mr. Carlson called out after them.

Kelsey pushed Steven down on her bed. "He doesn't know it's too late."

The lacy edges of her bra poked out from under her shirt, which made Steven happy. He couldn't understand why Denny didn't like women's breasts. Big, soft, round breasts. Kelsey kissed him enthusiastically and rubbed her hips over his, friction he could only stand for a moment before he moved her aside on the quilted bedspread.

"Don't start anything we can't finish," he warned.

"We can finish if we're quiet."

"And I'll be dead before we're done. What kind of gun does your dad have?"

"Just a little silver one." Kelsey pouted. "I don't think there's any bullets in it. Besides, you owe me. You ditched me last night."

"My brother nearly got killed."

"You didn't know he was in trouble," she reminded him. "You just like explosions. But I forgive you."

She rolled off the bed and then pulled something out from under it. She placed it squarely on his chest. "Look. Here's what I was talking about last night."

Steven glanced at the cover. It was gold and red and had some kind of drawing on it. A man on a swing? What? The title said *The Kama Sutra for Young Lovers.*

He pushed it aside. "Not now."

Kelsey dropped onto the mattress beside him. "Why not?"

Steven rolled onto his side to face her. "Because it's a long way to a cold shower. Did you see Lisa Horne at the party last night?"

She sighed. "With Eddie, sure. Is this about that boat?"

"Sort of. Did she stick around?"

"I don't know. She was dancing with that guy Brian Vandermark brought. I think that's why he got mad and picked that fight."

Which made sense. Eddie didn't usually go around insulting homosexuals, and he'd been very out of line with Brian and Denny.

Kelsey said, "Are you sure you don't want to take just one little look at the book? One or two pictures?"

"Maybe later," Steven said. Much, much later. Later as in never. Never, as in not while he still had breath in his body. Steven Anderson didn't need any Indian book of love to tell him how to do something he was already good at. The sooner Kelsey realized it, the better their relationship would be.

CHAPTER NINE

Denny's nap was rudely interrupted by someone knocking. After banging his shin on the coffee table, he swung the door open to see Brian standing on the porch. Brian's hair was loose and shaggy, his arms crossed over his chest. His wide blue eyes matched the blue of the sea behind him.

"What did you tell Christopher?" Brian asked.

"Huh?"

"He said you told him he was in trouble for lying to the police," Brian said unhappily. "That you were the sheriff's sons."

Brian was cute when he was upset. Denny remembered Lyle Horne's sneering words—*you and that pansy boy* —and told Lyle to get out of his head.

"The sheriff is down in Key West," Denny said.

"Not the point."

"Do you want to come in?"

Brian hesitated. "I guess."

Denny let him inside. He felt embarrassed, though. Obviously, the Vandermark family had money. They'd bought the second-biggest house on the island back at Christmas, and no doubt had filled it up with flat screen TVs, a home theater system, who knew what else. Meanwhile, neither of Denny's parents cared much about furniture. They bought stuff second-hand. Even their dishes and silverware came from thrift shops. The living room walls were covered with old fishing nets and Great-grandpa Clark's army medals, and the kitchen floor was nothing but cheap green linoleum. Usually Denny didn't care, but now he worried that it all looked shabby and cheap.

"You want a soda?" Denny asked.

Brian sat in a torn armchair. "No."

"Are you mad?"

"Not really. Well, not at you. He came in stoned last night, got my parents upset."

Denny grabbed a bottle of water and drank down half of it. "He's a good friend of yours. Christopher."

"Yeah."

"But he acts like a jerk."

Brian sighed. "I know."

"So why do you hang out with him?"

"I don't 'hang out' with anyone," Brian said. "He's just here until Monday. As a favor. And he wasn't always like this. He's just—well, never mind. Just don't talk to him, okay? We're going to Key West tonight for the weekend, and then he'll be out of here."

Denny said, "If you take him to Key West he's just going to ditch you on Duval Street."

"He won't—" Brian started, then stopped. "Maybe he will. But that's my problem, not yours."

Denny didn't answer. He'd figured out long ago that sometimes it was better to shut up than say things people might misinterpret. Things like, "You deserve better" and "He's just using you."

"He was my first," Brian blurted out. "And I guess that makes a difference."

Jealousy pinged through Denny like a submarine sonar blip—deep, clanging, impossible to ignore. Brian had done it with Christopher? Long-haired, shy, awkward Brian? While Denny was still the island's most frustrated virgin?

"You're turning pink," Brian said.

"Am not."

"You can ask questions if you want. My parents do."

Denny was mortified. "Why do your parents ask?"

"To make sure I stay safe," Brian said.

"I don't need to know anything," Denny said. So not true, though. He was pretty sure years of watching gay porn still wouldn't make him an expert when it came time to actually perform.

Christopher and Brian, though.

Brian deserved so much better.

"Forget I mentioned anything," Brian said. "What does it matter if Christopher and some others were at Beacon Point?"

"They found a duffel bag," Denny explained. "The guy who might have blown up *The Tempest* swam that way. Maybe it was his bag. If we find it, we might know more about him."

"Christopher says they didn't see any swimmers," Brian said. "Only Nathan Carter saw him. Maybe he's lying. Maybe he blew up the boat and then saved us so he wouldn't get charged with murder or something."

"Nathan Carter wouldn't need to stash a duffel bag at Beacon Point," Denny said. "He'd just swim back to his boat. Besides, someone piloted *The Tempest* into the harbor yesterday. That duffel bag is our only clue so far."

Brian's phone buzzed with a message. He skimmed it. "Christopher wants to get on the road to Key West."

"You don't have to go."

"Sure I do." Brian stood. "In case I didn't say it, last night was pretty awful."

Denny nodded.

"But awesome, too." Brian smiled. "When I leave for school, I'm going to remember last night more than anything else."

School, right. Brian and his nerdy friends at MIT, while Denny froze in the drafty halls of the Coast Guard Academy.

It occurred to Denny that this was the first and probably only time he'd be home alone with a gay guy. Mom and Dad were both at work, and Steven was probably off with Kelsey. It was the perfect time to admit the truth, throw himself on Brian's nice shoulder, and surrender everything.

Instead he watched Brian drive off, thought about how lucky and stupid Christopher was, and went to take his second shower of the day.

❖

Steven swung by the marina on his way home from Kelsey's. Nathan Carter was washing down the deck of his run-down boat. He was wearing a sleeveless T-shirt that showed off his muscles and a pair of long cargo shorts.

"Hey," Steven said from the dock.

Carter's eyes were hidden behind sunglasses. "Afternoon."

"Can I talk to you?"

"Sure. Come aboard."

There wasn't much for seating, just a padded bench and some folding lawn chairs. Carter pulled two ice-cold orange sodas from a red cooler and passed one over. A gift basket of chocolates and fruits was sitting on the cooler.

"Gift from the Vandermarks," Carter said.

"Nice," Steven said.

Carter said, "You're not the kid who nearly drowned. You're the brother."

"That's pretty good. People who've known us for years can't always tell us apart."

"They're not paying attention." Carter took a long drink from his soda. "They say you're going into SEAL training."

"Who says?"

Carter nodded toward the distant figure of Miss Nellie, still parked in her chair by the fence.

"Don't listen to all the town gossip," Steven said. "Did the police talk to you about *The Tempest*?"

"Sure. Last night and this morning. Maybe they think I had something to do with it instead of being a witness."

The boat rocked gently underneath them. Two seagulls whirled in search of food, maybe eyeing the gift basket. Steven drank his soda.

"Did you?"

Carter grinned without humor. "Sure. I thought she was so pretty that I wanted to blow her up. You know those ex-SEALs. Mentally unstable, no logic to them at all."

Steven's face burned a little. "Maybe there's logic we just don't know yet."

"Revenge?" Carter asked. "I knew the guy from way back and wanted to kill him. Money? Maybe somehow I get a cut of the insurance, if there's any insurance at all. Come on. Give me a motive."

Steven said, "The police have to ask."

"Sure they do. But they don't have to be stupid about it. If you're going to quiz me, kid, at least make it intelligent."

"I'm not going to quiz you. I don't think you did it."

Carter asked, "Why not?"

"Because you were a SEAL. If you did it, you would have been miles away when she blew up—not sticking around to rescue two kids."

"Good point."

Steven stood, leaving his half-empty soda behind. "But you still might be hiding something. Thanks for the drink."

He swung down to the dock, aware of Carter watching him. Steven got six feet away before Carter said, "Hey, kid."

"Yeah?"

"How come you don't want to know what it's like to be a SEAL? No questions at all? About BUD/S or anything?"

BUD/S was the special training school that Steven had been reading about for years. It was rigorous. Brutal. Designed to exhaust a man to the very inside of his bones, and still make him perform under pressure.

And it was totally out of Steven's reach.

"Today I just have questions about *The Tempest*," he said.

Carter leaned one foot on a railing. "I'll tell you about that boat. Leave it alone. If anything, that explosion was a message. It wasn't meant for you."

The breeze picked up, flapping lines and flags. Steven asked, "Was it meant for you?"

"I don't think so." Carter squinted off at the distant horizon. "But I've been wrong before."

CHAPTER TEN

Denny said, "Let's go to Key West tomorrow."

Steven squinted at the clock. Just after midnight. The noisy old air-conditioner wasn't doing much to cool their bedroom. Steven was annoyed, as usual, at how his feet hung over the end of his too-short bed. He needed a new bed. He needed to figure out what to do with his life.

"Why Key West?" he asked.

"Celebrate graduation. And we can go to karate class."

Just in general, Steven was never opposed to a trip down to Key West. Still, he said, "We both have to work on Sunday."

"Mom'll let me switch, and you can get someone to cover you."

Steven worked as a lifeguard at Fisher Key Resort, which he privately called "Hotel Most Likely to Overcharge You in Any Way Possible." The very nice sprawl of cottages and landscaping was the biggest resort between Key Largo and Key West. He really didn't understand why anyone would want to swim around a chlorinated pool when the entire Gulf of Mexico was just a few steps away, but the job paid well and the girls wore great bikinis.

"What about finding that duffel bag?" Steven asked.

"We can look for it first thing in the morning."

They rolled out of bed at sunrise and rowed over to Beacon Point to search among the mangroves. The crystal water was bathwater warm around Steven's ankles, with small silver fish darting around his every step. Denny had brought some garbage bags and they collected plastic bottles, soda cans and other trash as they waded along.

Steven could see the city marina from where they stood. The *Idle* was at her berth, but Nathan Carter didn't show himself.

"I still think he knows more than he's saying," he told Denny.

"Who?"

"Carter."

"I can't believe you went over there without me."

"You're just mad you couldn't lust over him in person. Forget it, Romeo. He's not gay."

"I never said he was." Denny scooped up a crushed plastic bottle. "How do you know?"

"I can tell."

"You can't always tell."

"Ninety-nine percent of the time, I can tell."

"Did you know about Brian Vandermark?"

"That's different. He never came to school. What, are you lusting over him now, too?"

"No," Denny said too quickly.

Steven wished he'd brought some coffee along. Or that he'd just stayed in bed. "You are. I can tell. Idiot. He has a boyfriend."

"It's not a boyfriend. It's an old friend."

"If you hang out with Brian all summer, people are going to gossip even more than they do right now."

"I don't care," Denny said, blatantly lying.

A glint of metal caught Steven's eye. He bent and fished a soggy green mess from under some roots. The duffel bag was about twenty inches long, nothing special about it, with a blank luggage tag and sturdy zipper. Nothing was inside it.

"Keep looking," Denny said.

Another hour of diligent searching produced nothing. Back home they hosed their legs down with a garden hose and hung the duffel bag up to dry. Their parents were in the kitchen, still in their bathrobes, kissing passionately against the sink.

"Morning, boys," Dad said when they were done. "Where've you been?"

"Fishing," Steven said.

Mom reached for her coffee. "Catch anything good?"

"Maybe," Denny said and explained the duffel bag while Steven made breakfast for everyone.

"Even if it belonged to our mystery swimmer, it's still a bag full of nothing," Dad said when Denny was done. "Unless we can ID it somehow, it can't lead anywhere."

Steven served up plates of golden-fried French toast with butter and syrup. "We'll keep looking for a tie."

Denny fetched silverware from the drawer. "Do you guys care if we go down to Key West today?"

"You're supposed to work tomorrow," Mom said.

Denny flashed her a smile. "I'm hoping the boss will let me off."

"What are you going to do in Key West?" Dad asked.

Steven said, "Drive responsibly, be helpful toward the elderly, and avoid underage drinking."

Dad rolled his eyes. "Or are you going down to dig around in this case? You know what I've told you about leaving the police work to the police."

"Not that it seems to sink in," Mom observed.

"You tell us that all the time, but then we catch the bad guys and everything turns out well," Steven said.

"True," Dad said. "Where will you stay?"

Denny poured orange juice for himself. "Sensei Mike will let us sleep in the dojo."

Mom wrinkled her nose. "That hard floor."

"Good for the spine," Steven said.

Dad said, "I suppose it's okay. Remember, Mom and I are going up to Tallahassee next week for that state conference. Get your wild oats in now. But promise you'll stay out of trouble."

"Promise."

"Double promise."

"And one more thing," Dad said.

"Yes, Dad?" they asked in unison.

Dad held out his plate. "More French toast, please."

❖

The road to Key West was a straight shot across the Seven Mile Bridge and down the Overseas Highway. They had driven it enough times to do it blindfolded, but every small town had a stoplight or two, and every bridge required a drop in the speed limit, and an afternoon squall drenched the two-lane road. They drank soda and argued over the radio station for two hours.

"Tell me why we're really on this road trip," Steven finally said, drumming his fingers on the steering wheel.

Denny wasn't about to admit anything about Brian Vandermark. "To celebrate. Nothing else."

"You're hiding something."

"Says you. You've been hiding something since that freak-out at graduation."

"I didn't freak out. It was claustrophobia."

"You better get over that before BUD/S."

Steven didn't answer.

Denny swiveled in the passenger seat and said, "That's it. You're freaking out about BUD/S!"

"Keep saying I'm freaking out and you can walk the rest of the way," Steven threatened.

Denny smirked. "I'm totally right."

"You're totally a moron."

By the time they reached Key West the rain had tapered off, but traffic was slow because of waterlogged roads. New Town was Denny's least favorite part of the island—concrete and strip malls, cheap motels, and liquor stores. They followed a tourist trolley for a half mile, then got stuck behind a tour bus. The sun came out and made the pavements sizzle.

"If I'm ever a tourist, shoot me," Steven said.

Conch Nation Martial Arts was on White Street, in a former coffee mill with white clapboard siding and large blue shutters. A dozen women were doing yoga stretches inside, sweating in the breeze of ceiling fans. Steven wanted to linger, but Denny dragged him around to the cottage in the back.

One quick knock and Denny pushed the door open. "Sensei! We're home."

Sensei Mike Kahalepuna was in the living room, swinging a remote control at the TV in a virtual game of tennis. The room was full of bamboo furniture and South Pacific tribal masks, and a dozen cats were making themselves at home on any available flat surface.

"Boys!" Sensei Mike said, rolling toward them in his wheelchair. "Did you graduate?"

"With honors," Denny said, and bent down for a hug.

"He tells that to everyone," Steven said, his hug next.

Sensei Mike turned off the game. He'd lost more hair since their last visit, or maybe it migrated from his head to his beefy forearms. He'd been a Marine in Iraq before returning home and losing his legs in a car accident. Denny had never heard him complain, never.

"High school graduates," Sensei Mike mused. "You must be full of wisdom."

"I am." Steven sat on the oversized sofa. "My brother's still dumber than a rock."

"A rock that can kick your butt in sparring," Denny said.

Sensei Mike grinned. "Class isn't until seven tomorrow. Then we'll see who can kick what. What's the plan until then?"

Denny sat on the floor and petted a black cat. "Time-share presentations."

"T-shirt shops."

"Virgin daiquiris."

"Virgins," Steven said.

A tabby cat made her way to Denny's lap. "And we might check out a guy named Nathan Carter. He spent the winter down here."

"Name's not familiar. Tell me more."

"Used to be a SEAL, has a crap fishing boat, and likes to swim around the ocean at night," Steven said.

Sensei Mike's expression brightened. "Big guy, blond, gay?"

Denny grinned triumphantly. "I knew it!"

"Not gay," Steven said.

"Totally gay," Sensei Mike said. "Not very vocal about it, though."

Steven frowned. "Then how do you know?"

"He had a boyfriend," Sensei Mike said. "Square law-and-order type."

Denny's imagination was already working overtime—him, Carter, and Brian, all of them sailing around the tropics on Carter's boat, marathon sex on the white sands of St. Thomas.

"I knew it," Denny said.

"You did not," Steven replied crossly. "Just because you're gay yourself doesn't mean you can automatically tell when someone else is. That's a myth."

Denny blinked.

Had Steven just said that in front of Sensei Mike?

Yes, he had.

Which meant that for the first time in his life, Denny had been outed.

CHAPTER ELEVEN

S teven felt like the worst brother in the world.
Denny was gaping at him in disbelief. Sensei Mike wasn't
saying anything at all. Steven wanted to grab up the last few minutes
and erase them from everyone's memory. He couldn't believe he'd
actually said the words in front of an adult.

"That was a joke," he said hastily.

Denny blinked and looked away.

Sensei Mike cleared his throat. "Well, joke or not, sometimes
you can guess, and sometimes you can't. I think Carter's used to
hiding it. He had to, in the military. Down here—well, you know.
Things are looser."

"It's not a joke," Denny said, the words rushed. His gaze was
solely on the tabby cat in his lap. "What he said."

Steven let out a long breath. He hated the uncertainty in Denny's
voice. That for the rest of his life he was going to have to decide who
to tell, how to tell them, whether he could trust them. It was easy for
Steven. He was what people assumed him to be. But for Denny the
wrong choice could mean losing a job or friendship or worse.

Sensei Mike tilted his head. "Does it make a difference?"

Denny kept patting the cat. "To some people."

"You think it makes a difference to me?"

For a moment, the only sound was the Indian music from the
yoga class through the open windows. Denny looked up and met
Sensei Mike's gaze squarely.

"I hope not."

Sensei Mike sighed. "You really are dumber than a rock. I don't care what floats your boat, Denny. Where you stick your oar. What port you put into. Need I go on with bad puns?"

"Please don't." Steven grimaced.

Denny didn't smile, but he said, "They're not puns. They're euphemisms."

"Great. I'm glad we know our parts of speech." Sensei Mike clapped his hands together. "Now, how about a late lunch? I made a new recipe. Asparagus casserole. With goat cheese."

The casserole was pretty good, Steven admitted. Lunch was kind of awkward, and he wasn't quite sure what to say without sticking his foot down his throat again. Denny and Sensei Mike carried the conversation with talk about students in the dojo. Afterward Sensei Mike gave them his spare keys and went off in his custom-made van to visit his girlfriend.

"Don't wait up for me," he said.

When they were alone in the living room Steven said, "Let's go down to the waterfront to find out more about Nathan Carter."

"You go. There's something I want to run down."

"Something like what?"

"Something private," Denny said, his voice hard. "Remember that thing? Privacy?"

"I'm sorry! It just came out. I didn't even realize what I was saying," Steven pleaded. "It was stupid."

"Yes. Stupid and thoughtless," Denny said. Then he sighed. "But he took it okay, right?"

"Of course he did. You were worried?"

"I worry all the time," Denny replied. "Forget it. You go down to the waterfront. I'll catch up with you."

Steven hesitated.

"Go." Denny waved his hand. "Keep in touch."

"You, too," Steven said. He wasn't sure what secret Denny was hiding now, but he didn't like it. Didn't like it all.

CHAPTER TWELVE

Denny couldn't be mad at Steven. Well, sure he could. Stupid, infuriating, idiotic Steven, who'd announced Denny was gay to the one person who definitely did not need to know. Not that Sensei Mike was homophobic or anything, but he was a former Marine, and a black belt about a dozen times over, and he'd been their teacher for almost four years. He didn't need to know where Denny wanted to put his oar.

Dumb euphemism, he thought.

Still, Sensei Mike hadn't seemed upset, and he definitely hadn't seemed surprised. So things could have been a lot worse.

Steven was still an idiot, though.

After Steven left, Denny hauled out Sensei Mike's phone book and started calling hotels. The easiest thing to do was get Brian's number from his mom back on Fisher Key and then just call Brian directly. But he didn't want to look like some weird stalker. He just wanted to check up on things. Make sure Brian was okay. Make sure Christopher wasn't treating him like dirt.

The fourth hotel was the Casa Marina, and the operator said yes, she'd put him through to Brian Vandermark. He hung up before the room phone began to ring. Better to just go over there himself.

He washed up in the bathroom, combed his hair, and eyed himself in the mirror.

"I just happened to be swinging through," he might say to Brian.

Or, "Hey, I didn't think I'd see you here."

He hoped he didn't sound too dumb.

Sensei Mike kept an old moped in the back for guests—bright yellow but with a quiet engine, immaculately maintained. Denny drove over to the hotel and parked a block away. The Casa Marina was a beautiful old building that had once belonged to the famous tycoon Henry Flagler. You couldn't grow up in Florida and escape history lessons about him, his railroads and hotels, and how he'd changed the future of the Florida Keys.

But Denny wasn't interested in history right now. He passed through the ornate lobby as confidently as any registered guest and went outside again. Acres of careful landscaping surrounded an enormous pool, all of it fronting a private beach of white sand. It didn't take long to spy Brian and Christopher standing knee-deep in the blue and green sea. They were bare-chested and laughing, their skin gleaming with suntan lotion.

Christopher reached over and planted a kiss on Brian's shoulder, then shoved him into the waves. Brian surfaced, laughing, his hair slicked back behind him.

Horrible jealousy swept over Denny. Who got to live like that? Kissing and laughing in the sun and not worrying about who saw you? Just another beautiful Saturday afternoon in the sun and you could kiss your boyfriend if you wanted to.

But not if you didn't dare have a boyfriend at all.

He went back to his moped with the vague idea that life would just be better if he drove himself off the Seven Mile Bridge. Then he'd never have to worry about the virgin thing, or the gay thing, or the fact he was never going to fall in love with anyone, or anyone with him.

He sped away from the Casa Marina, his hands steering even if his brain was full of Christopher kissing Brian's shoulder. Without really thinking about it, he found himself on a dead-end lane near Simonton Street. Jimmy Buffet music floated over a nearby fence, along with the sounds of clinking glasses, splashing water, and men laughing. The fence had a gated door with the logo of a giant blue goose on it, and the porch of the adjacent house was decorated with an enormous rainbow flag.

He knew all about the Blue Goose. He'd been visiting their website for years. He knew how many rooms it had, how they were decorated, what he could expect to pay in the off-season. What the pool looked like. What the naked men lounging by the pool would probably look like as they smoothed oil over one another's skin.

He didn't believe in Paradise, exactly, but the Blue Goose was a place where you could look at other men, and be openly affectionate, and do all sorts of things without people looking at you in disgust or dismay.

"Going in?" asked a voice.

Denny turned. The man in the street behind him was handsome in a middle-aged kind of way, with a British accent that made him sound dashing and suave. With the man was a black-and-brown terrier on the edge of a leash. The terrier sniffed at a nearby hydrant and lifted its leg.

"No," Denny said quickly. "I'm not here—I mean, I'm lost. I'm looking for Mallory Square."

The British man smiled. His green shirt was unbuttoned near the neck and tight khaki shorts clung to his long legs.

"I was lost once," he said. "Wandered around the wilderness for years."

"There's not much wilderness here.

"Metaphorical, I'll say. How old are you?"

Denny's mouth dried out a little. "Twenty-one."

"Then you should come inside and have a drink, Mr. I'm Not Lost. No one in there bites. Not unless you want them to."

"I'm not—" Denny stopped halfway through the sentence.

"Not lost?" The British man asked gently. "Not wandering?"

"I have to go." Denny started the moped up again. "Thanks anyway."

He sped off toward Mallory Square, never once looking back.

❖

Steven spent a frustrating afternoon visiting marinas and boatyards, looking for information about Nathan Carter. Most people he talked to didn't know him. Hardly a surprise, given the transient nature of boaters. He had better luck with some live-aboards near Key West bight who remembered Carter but had nothing interesting to say about him. He was quiet, kept to himself, and drank sometimes down at the Crazy Parrot.

The bartender at the Crazy Parrot was a big girl who had once been a big guy, or so it seemed to Steven. The fake ID that had been working for a year now got Steven a beer just as the sun was setting low in the palm trees. The back porch overlooked a courtyard with a koi pond in it. White Christmas lights had been strung up inside, along the rafters. *Almost like stars*, Steven thought, but he preferred the real sky and real stars.

He messaged Eddie again, was pissed when there was no response. Called him, but got voice mail. After a few minutes of debate, he called Eddie's house and reached Mrs. Ibarra.

"Eddie's up in Miami," she said, sounding weary. "He must have lost his phone again."

She was a woman who'd had nothing but misfortune for most of her life—Eddie's father being a drunk, Eddie's father leaving them, her own bad health. Steven knew she worked at Sal's Gas & Go and had recently started cleaning houses, too. There was never much money in the house, especially for trips to Miami. But Lisa Horne had some money, and Steven thought that was why Eddie was dating her.

"Tell him I called, please," Steven said to Mrs. Ibarra. "Thanks."

Slowly the bar filled up with locals. Somewhere around Steven's third beer, a blond girl in a sparkly blue T-shirt slid onto the stool beside him.

"Tourist or local?" she asked.

"Local."

"Good," she said, and tucked a curl behind her right ear. She was pretty and toned. Yoga instructor, he decided. Maybe Pilates. Easily six or seven years older than he was, but he wasn't going to tell her. "I'm Bethany."

"I'm Steven. Can I get you something?"

She wanted a beer and so he got her one. She told him she worked as a waitress at Sloppy Joe's, the biggest tourist bar on the island. And she taught yoga. Score one for him. Between songs she slipped her hand onto his knee. Score two.

"What do you do?" she asked.

"I just graduated," he said. "University of Miami."

That was a stretch, but she didn't seem to notice. Or maybe she did. Hard to tell with women, sometimes. She said she'd moved down after graduating with an art degree in North Carolina.

"Do you know what you can do with an art degree?" she asked.

"Not a lot. But this seems like as good a place as any, if you're not going to do a lot. I love this town. And hate my roommates."

"Yeah, I know how that goes."

"You have a roommate?"

"Sure. He snores a lot and doesn't wash his sheets enough. Once he brought home a snake and kept it under his bed for a month."

Bethany leaned closer. Her eyebrows were very thin, her bustline very high. He wondered if those breasts were real. Two girls at Fisher Key High had already gotten boob jobs. "Is he home now? My roommates are both home."

Score three.

He told himself Kelsey was probably home reading the *Kama Sutra* right this minute. On her quilted bedspread surrounded by her teddy bears. Whereas he was, well, he was practicing. Exactly what she'd encouraged him to do.

They'd never promised monogamy, after all.

Bethany's gaze slid past him to the doorway. "Hey. He looks just like you."

Steven didn't have to turn around to figure out that Denny had walked in. "Nah. Whoever he is, he's ugly."

Bethany grinned. "You have a twin?"

"Clone," Steven said. "Made in a Chinese factory. But they forgot to put in a brain, so forgive him if he sounds stupid."

Denny sidled up right beside Bethany and ordered his own beer. He looked morose. Steven hoped he still wasn't mad about the accidental-outing thing. Hours had passed. Get over it.

"Hi," Bethany said to Denny. "Your brother says you're a clone."

Denny's voice was dry. "I'm the original. He's an alien pod from Planet X."

"I like you both," she said and scooted off her stool. "Be right back."

Steven watched her head off to the ladies' room before turning back to Denny. "How'd you get here?"

"Same way you did. Asked around. Anyone here know Nathan Carter?"

"I haven't asked."

Denny snagged the bartender. "We're trying to track down a friend of ours. Nathan Carter. You know him?"

The bartender pursed her cherry-red lips. "Nope."

"He used to drink here," Steven said.

She tossed her hair. "So did Ernest Hemingway. There's a plaque on the wall that says so. But I never knew him."

A customer called her down to the other end of the bar. Denny swallowed his beer and said, "Not so surprising. No one wants to talk about Carter. What's with the girl?"

"What about her? You promised me a celebration and this is it, my celebration," Steven said. "Do you think Sensei Mike will mind if we use the dojo?"

Denny made his famous sour face. "What about Kelsey?"

"Shut up."

"She saved herself for you. And here you are, cheating behind her back—"

"She didn't save herself!" Steven exclaimed, then lowered his voice. "She promised her dad. I'm just the guy she picked to help her break her vow."

Denny shrugged.

"I hate you," Steven said, sliding off his stool.

"Yeah, I know. Voice of your conscience."

They left the Crazy Parrot before Bethany could return. Outside, the air smelled like jasmine and the neon lights over Sloppy

Joe's flashed against the dark sky. Steven wished he really had just graduated from the University of Miami. That he had a diploma and some career that would fill up the emptiness of not being a SEAL.

"Where's your truck?" Denny asked, his voice low against the laughter and music drifting from bars.

"About four blocks from here."

"Huh."

"What?"

"Don't look now, but I think we're being followed."

CHAPTER THIRTEEN

Steven turned around and looked down the sidewalk. Lovers strolled hand in hand, young women stood clustered on the sidewalk with beer cups in hand, and a trickle of people waited at an ice cream stand. Just another balmy night in paradise.

"Who's following us?" he asked loudly.

"You could be more subtle," Denny complained.

"It's not my style."

A man turned toward them from the window of a jewelry shop. "Obviously not," he said. He was an Hispanic man in his early thirties, swarthy and athletic. He was dressed casually in gray slacks and a white polo shirt, with expensive gray shoes.

In the Secret Yearbook—or whatever it was now, since graduation—Steven tagged him as Most Likely to Waste His Money.

"Can we help you with something?" Steven asked.

The man closed the distance between them. His hands hung loose at his sides and his shoulders were relaxed, but he looked like the kind of man who'd hit fast and hard in a fight.

"I heard some guys were asking questions about a friend of mine," the man said. "But you're just teenagers."

Denny bristled. "We're older than we look."

"I doubt it," the man replied. Cool, calm. Steven didn't see a gun on him, but the possibility certainly existed. The man asked, "What do you want with Nathan Carter?"

"Who's he to you?" Steven asked.

"A friend. What do you want with him?"

Denny said, "He saved my life. That inspires a little curiosity."

Something flickered in the man's eyes—amusement, maybe. "He likes to save lives. But he doesn't like questions. My advice to you is that you stop."

"My advice is that you don't worry about it," Steven said.

The man smiled slightly. It was the smile of a man putting down a winning hand at poker.

He said, "Or maybe you'd like me to confiscate those fake IDs of yours and give them to your dad up in Fisher Key. Is Captain Anderson a big fan of underage drinking?"

❖

Brian had never been to the gay bars of Key West before that weekend. He'd only been to one gay bar in his whole life, in fact, and that had been a depressing hole-in-the-wall in New Hampshire full of middle-aged men and weak beer. So the Priscilla Ann Saloon was an entirely new experience: murals of drag queens on the wall, tropical drinks with obscenely shaped straws, and boisterous street signs behind the bar such as "Drama Queen Lane." Loud music—tech, disco, and tech-disco combined—pounded through the speakers and over the thick crowd.

It was the kind of place where you could shove your tongue down another man's throat and get cheered, not jeered.

Which is why he was standing in the corner, thumbing through pages on his phone. Christopher was off dancing with anyone he could snag.

Christopher was always off dancing, Brian thought with a sigh.

"Hey, baby girl," said the bartender. "Don't just stand there! Get your groove on. Don't surf the net when you've got the real thing in front of you."

Brian hadn't been able to replace his waterlogged phone before leaving for Key West, so Henrik had loaned him his spare. It had a much better Web browser. He was looking up newspaper accounts of Denny and Steven Anderson, Fisher Key's homegrown heroes.

MYSTERY OF THE TEMPEST

"I'm fine," he told the bartender, meaning *Leave Me Alone*.

"Sweetie, you're very fine, but get that ass out there. Don't gloom up the place."

Brian stepped outside instead. It was cooler out there and a lot quieter. This was the third bar they'd been to tonight, plus two they'd visited last night. Bars were not Brian's style. Christopher called him "repressed," but Brian preferred "serious." Or maybe "cautious." Or maybe just "boring."

He texted Christopher that he had a headache and would meet him back at the hotel. The walk was only a half-mile along the pleasant streets. Gay and straight couples passed by, nuzzling each other's necks and drinking from each other's cups. He imagined what it would be like to walk with a lover, the two of them young and invincible against everything the future held.

His lover would look just like Denny Anderson. Denny, with his dark hair and dark eyes and way of looking right into you, like he knew your every secret.

Did Denny close his eyes when he kissed?

Brian had always been good at torturing himself.

His phone buzzed. He hoped for a reply from Christopher, but instead it was his mother: *Having fun? Love you. Call in the morning.*

He was halfway through the handsome lobby of the Casa Marina when he almost bumped into an elderly lady who was talking on her cell phone. "Sorry," she said, giving him a little pat on the arm.

At the same time, a gray-haired man in a suit rose from a chair by the elevator and asked, "Brian Vandermark?"

"Yes."

The man flashed a badge. "I'm Agent James Prosper, Miami FBI."

Brian's heartbeat quickened. He'd never talked to the FBI before. "Kind of late hours for the FBI, isn't it?"

"You're telling me." Prosper chuckled. His clothes were rumpled and circles hung under his eyes. "But if I can grab some moments of your time now, I can be home when my kid wakes up in the morning. It's his birthday."

"Okay," Brian said. "Should we talk in private? My room?"

"No. We can do it here."

They sat on two sofas not far from the front desk. Prosper took a moleskin notebook from the inside pocket of his jacket. "I talked to your parents and they said you were here. They're still a little shaken up by what happened the other night."

"It wasn't much, really. We were just in the wrong place at the wrong time."

"If you could tell me the story in your own words, that would be great."

So Brian retold the tale, trying to think of any details that he might have left out in the police report at Fisher Key. Prosper nodded and took notes and occasionally stifled a yawn.

When Brian was done, Prosper said, "You have a friend staying with you. He saw the explosion from shore?"

"Christopher Morgan. He's not here right now."

"But he saw it?"

"Yes. Him and some others. They were at Beacon Point."

"And they found a suitcase of some kind?"

"A duffel bag, I think. You'd have to ask him."

"It might be a clue," Prosper said. "Any little thing might help. This Christopher Morgan…he's your boyfriend?"

The words were casual, but a little forced.

"Not right now," Brian said.

Prosper sounded rueful. "I know how that goes. My wife, twelve years we're together. Then she leaves me for our kid's orthodontist. Your parents are okay with it? You being gay?"

Brian stared at him. "I don't see what—"

"It's just that my kid? Plays with dolls. He's seven. Dresses them up, changes their diapers, puts them down for naps. My ex-wife says it's a stage. I say we have to get it out of him now, before it's too late. It's not like when you have two sons, and one can carry on your legacy while the other does what he wants. Right?"

The words "get it out of him now" made goose bumps rise on Brian's neck. Maybe Prosper didn't realize what it made him sound like. Maybe he was tired, words slipping out before he could really think about them.

Or maybe not.

"Just one kid, but he's mine," Prosper continued. "I'd kill for him if I had to. Nothing I wouldn't do. Your dad probably feels the same way."

"Henrik's my stepdad."

"Would he protect you?"

"Protect me from what?"

Prosper smiled crookedly. "Everyone needs protection from something, kid."

Brian was suddenly glad he hadn't brought Prosper up to his room. He stood up. "It's kind of late. I need to go now."

"Sure, kid." Prosper tucked his notebook away. "I'll come back in the morning to talk to your friend."

Brian nodded and left him there by the sofas. He could feel Prosper's gaze on him all the way to the elevators, and how creepy was that? He listened for footsteps on the tile but heard only the ringing of a phone at the front desk and the muted TV hanging in a lounge area. His hand went to his pocket and touched the reassuring weight of his cell phone. If something happened he could call 911—

Nothing happened. He got onto the elevator and punched the button for the third floor without looking to see if Prosper was still watching him. The closing of the doors brought enormous relief.

Get it out of him.

Would your parents protect you?

The long hallway on the third floor was empty. Brian felt for his key card, but his pocket was empty. What? He checked his other pocket. It held only his phone and small wallet. Damn it. He must have dropped the card at the gay bar or somewhere on the way home.

He'd have to turn around and get a new one.

Then he saw that his door was open, wedged ajar by the deadbolt. Light spilled out from inside.

Brian opened the door carefully. "Christopher? Did you—"

He didn't finish. The room was empty. The pillows and bedsheets were on the floor, all twisted up. The drawers of the bureau had been pulled open and the clothes torn out. All of their toiletries had been dumped on the bathroom counter and some bottles had fallen to floor, spilling blue and green gel on the white tile.

He stared in disbelief.

They'd been robbed.

CHAPTER FOURTEEN

Sleeping on the dojo floor wasn't fun, but with some mats for padding it wasn't all bad.

"I can't believe that guy was a cop," Denny complained in the darkness.

"Notice he didn't show us his badge," Steven said. "He could have been anyone."

"I think he was telling the truth."

"I think he was a jerk."

In the morning, fifteen Okinawan kenpo students showed up in their white gi uniforms for class. Some adults, some kids, three women. As the most senior brown belts, Steven and Denny took their places in the second row. Steven watched himself constantly in the mirror, checking his form. Ninety minutes of push-ups, kicks, punches and blocks left him drenched with sweat, just the way he liked it.

The regular class ended, but the black belts stayed around for more sparring. At the end of it, Steven, Denny, and Sensei Mike went to breakfast at the Cuban diner down the street.

"So when do you go to the academy?" Sensei Mike asked Denny.

"Next month for training."

"And boot camp for you, Steven?"

Steven swallowed some scalding hot coffee. Of all the people he hated to lie to, Sensei Mike was high on the list. "September."

"He's worried about BUD/S," Denny said.

"You're stupendously wrong. I've got nothing to worry about."

Sensei Mike forked some of his ham croqueta. "Bravery is one thing, bravado is another. If BUD/S doesn't scare you, either you don't know what you're getting into or it's not worth going."

Steven watched a dark-haired waitress bend over at the next table. He liked the way her white blouse pulled across her chest, and looking at her was easier than looking at Sensei Mike.

"Maybe I'm just ignorant," he quipped.

"I'll second that," Denny said. "Don't worry. When you wash out, maybe they'll keep you around to swab the decks."

Steven decided to change the subject before he felt even guiltier about lying. "Can we test for black belt before we go?"

Sensei Mike studied them both. "You think you're ready?"

"Never more ready," Denny said.

"I could do it today," Steven added.

"Oh, to be eighteen years old again," Sensei Mike said with a laugh.

Steven's phone rang. He didn't recognize the number. "Hello?"

"Um, hi. This is Brian Vandermark. I was looking for Denny."

Steven passed the phone over and said, "What am I? Your secretary?"

Denny asked, "Hello?" and listened intently for a moment. Then he said, "Okay, stay there. We came down for karate class, so we'll be right over."

When he hung up Steven asked, "We'll be right over where?"

"Casa Marina," Denny said, frowning. "Someone broke into his room last night."

"Sounds like your kind of case," Sensei Mike said and signaled for the check.

❖

Brian and Christopher's room at the Casa Marina was nicely furnished with modern furniture, sleek lighting, and a king-sized bed. Denny tried not to think about the bed or what they'd been doing in it.

"Swank," Steven said. "How much does it cost to stay here?"

"Ignore him," Denny told Brian. "This was ransacked?"

Brian pushed his glasses up on his nose. He was wearing a thin blue jersey and swimming trunks, although he looked too worried to be considering an afternoon by the pool. "No. They moved us here last night after Christopher threw a hissy fit. Our original room is on the third floor, but I don't know if we can get in it."

"You said the door was open when you got back. No signs it was forced open?" Denny asked.

"No. The manager said whoever got in must have had a key. I must have lost mine, but how would someone know what room to use it on? They're not marked."

Steven plopped down in an armchair by the balcony doors. "You lost it, or it was stolen?"

Brian look confused. "I was pick-pocketed?"

"Maybe."

Denny poked his head into the hallway and looked for security cameras. None.

"So where's Douchebag?" Steven asked.

Brian winced. "Please don't call him that."

"Okay. Where's Mr. Personality?"

A sigh. "Down at the pool. Working on his suntan."

Denny wanted to wipe the strained expression off Brian's face. No, what he really wanted was to give him a reassuring hug.

But not in front of Steven.

"Did the hotel report it to the police?"

"No. They apologized and offered us a few extra nights if we stayed quiet," Brian said. "Wanted to avoid the publicity, I guess. All they got was about a hundred dollars in cash."

"So why'd you call us?" Steven asked.

"Everyone says you help solve crimes," Brian said. "A second opinion would be nice."

"It could just be a crime of opportunity," Denny said.

"And nothing to do with the boat that blew up?" Brian asked.

Steven put his feet up on an ottoman. "Nah. Just a lot of bad luck."

Brian sat on the edge of the bed. "There was an FBI agent here last night, asking about it. Agent Prosper. He wanted to know about Christopher and the bag that was found at Beacon Point. He was kind of a creep."

"How much of a creep?" Denny asked.

"Said some weird things about his own son, and if he was gay he was going to have to 'get it out of him.' Like, I don't know. An exorcism? A beating? Then he asked about my stepfather. And was just weird."

Denny asked, "Did you get his name? See his badge?"

"Yes, he showed me his badge. James Prosper from the Miami office. Why?"

"If he was a real jerk you could complain to the field office," Denny said.

"I don't think I want to do that. But he was supposed to come back this morning, and he hasn't shown up yet."

"Maybe we'll stick around," Denny said. "See how much of a creep he really is."

"Stick around?" Steven protested.

Brian looked relieved. "Can you do that?"

"Sure," Denny said. "Class is over, and we've got nothing better to do all day."

Steven said, "I might have better things to do."

Denny gave him a pointed look and put his best effort into twin ESP.

Steven looked mutinous.

Brian spoke up. "They have WaveRunners we could rent. And there's a reef trip for snorkeling. Plus windsurfing."

Denny admired Brian for knowing exactly what would appeal to Steven. Steven glanced between the two of them and then shrugged.

"You had me at WaveRunners," he said.

CHAPTER FIFTEEN

Christopher didn't seem pleased to have company, and it didn't help that he kept dumping his Runner into the ocean. Denny didn't worry too much about Christopher, though. He was having too much fun speeding along the coastline. Steven went full-out, daring the waves and his machine both. Show-off. Denny hung back and taught Brian how to jump some of the smaller waves. Every time Brian laughed or smiled, Denny felt equally happy. Sun, water, and a cute guy by his side. It was like Denny had won the jackpot.

After a few hours they circled back to the resort to have lunch in the hotel restaurant. While serving up their hamburgers, the waitress mentioned there was a snorkeling trip to the reef leaving at three o'clock.

"Sunset tour," she promised. "Very pretty. You can sign up at the front desk."

She was an attractive dark-haired woman, and Steven watched her walk away with obvious interest. Denny ignored him.

"I've never snorkeled," Brian confessed. "Don't you need to be certified?"

"Not for sticking on a mask and a plastic tube," Steven said. "It's easy."

Christopher said, "Rubber makes me itch."

Steven opened his mouth as if to say something. Denny kicked him under the table.

"You're getting a little sunburned," Brian told Christopher. "Do you feel it?"

Christopher touched his nose. "Maybe. We should stay here, out of the sun. We could go to the movies or something."

Steven said, "No one comes to Key West to go to the movies."

Denny didn't like the cheerful tone of his voice. Yes, it was clear Steven didn't like Christopher much, but something else was going on. His twin was scheming about something.

"What do you think?" Brian asked Denny.

Denny didn't want to be part of Steven's machinations, but he couldn't lie. "Sure. A day like today? Great visibility. It'll be beautiful."

"You should all go," Steven said. "I'll meet you back at the dojo."

"I'm tired," Christopher complained.

Denny saw Steven's plan now. He stood up and dropped his napkin onto his chair. "Steven and I will go check to see if there are any reservations left."

"We will?" Steven asked.

Denny walked out of the restaurant. Steven followed him. Denny found a small coat room area near the restaurant and pushed Steven into it.

"What are you doing?" he demanded.

Steven spread his hands innocently. "What?"

"Last week you were complaining if I even looked at a guy. Now you're trying to set me up on this snorkel trip with Brian. What are you, schizophrenic?"

"Relax!" Steven said. "I was wrong. You need some company. He's gay, you're gay, he likes you, you like—"

"Inside voice!" Denny snapped.

Steven dropped his voice. "You're leaving next month. You sit around and do nothing but mope around, I'll kill you. For my sake, go out with him."

Denny almost believed him. But then he said, "No. This is you trying to make up for spilling it to Sensei Mike."

"So what? I'm your brother. I want you to be happy."

"You need to stay out of it," Denny said sternly. "I don't want your advice and I don't want you meddling."

Steven leaned forward. "I don't meddle! I fix things that you screw up. So stop screwing up."

Denny shook his head.

"Excuse me," Brian said, from about five feet away. His expression was inscrutable, and it was impossible for Denny to know how much he'd overheard. "I'm ready to go snorkeling if you are."

Steven patted Denny's shoulder. "Call me when you get back."

Denny wanted to punch him, but instead he let Steven leave.

Brian asked, "Are you okay?"

"Yes," Denny said. "Fine. You sure you want to go out? Christopher won't be pissed?"

"He's already pissed," Brian said, briefly glancing back to the restaurant. "But that's his problem. He thinks you're gay, but I told him you're not. That we're just friends. And I want to learn how to snorkel."

"Oh," Denny said. "Okay."

The worst part of it was that Brian sounded like he absolutely believed Denny was straight. And he didn't sound disappointed about it either. Maybe he was glad Denny wasn't available. Maybe there was some incredible deficiency in Denny's character that meant no reasonable guy would ever want to sleep with him.

For the sake of his own sanity, Denny ought to follow Steven right out of the hotel.

"Ready?" Brian asked.

"Sure. Lead on."

CHAPTER SIXTEEN

W hat about sharks?" one of the women on the boat asked.
The captain smiled. "Nothing to worry about."

Brian looked over at Denny.

"You're not going to get eaten by sharks," Denny said. "I promise."

Still, the idea had been planted. Treading water in the waves, surrounded by miles of sea and sky, Brian tried not to think about killer animals with razor-sharp teeth that might snatch off one of his legs or arms. Instead, he concentrated on breathing through the snorkel and keeping his mask from fogging up.

"Relax," Denny said. "You'll love it."

He led the way across the reef, and Brian told himself *no sharks, no sharks, no sharks.*

The underwater world was—oh.

Beautiful.

Colorful fish zigzagged across fields of red and brown coral like a nature documentary surrounding him in 3-D on all sides. *The world's biggest theater*, he thought to himself. Sea plants and grass waved in the currents. Purple plants, green plants—some he recognized as anemones, and others looked as exotic as something from another planet. Denny taught him to submerge, hold his breath, then clear his snorkel and breathe without breaking all the way up into the world of air.

He felt a pang of regret that he hadn't done this months ago.

And every once in a while he looked for sharks, but mostly he trusted Denny to let him know if anything bad was about to happen.

Denny, with his amazingly long and lean body, and that crinkle around his eyes when he was amused, and the way he'd just shown up when Brian needed him.

Which was kind of a big coincidence. He'd called their house on Fisher Key and their mother had told him they were down in Key West for karate. Denny hadn't mentioned anything about that when Brian saw him on Friday. Maybe it had been a last-minute thing.

That didn't quite explain the argument Steven and Denny had been having in the coat room. Brian had overheard only a little of it, but enough to intrigue him.

Was Denny gay after all?

Because now that he thought about it, Brian hadn't seen Denny ogling any girls today. He hadn't seemed at all interested in them. Unlike Steven, who couldn't keep his eyes in his head half the time.

In the swirl of sea, color, and fish, Brian pretended Denny was his boyfriend and that they'd come to Key West together on vacation. That they'd be spending the night in that big bed upstairs. Some good should come out of it. Brian and Christopher's first room had contained two queen beds, but the king had been the only thing available in the middle of the night.

Yes, he liked this fantasy. He and Denny would spend the night together, and Brian would teach Denny how to have sex with another guy.

At sunset they climbed back into the boat. The captain did a quick count to make sure no one had been left behind. Denny was quiet all the way back to the resort, with no outward sign of what he was thinking. Brian sat close beside him, just as silent. Nearby was the woman who'd been worried about sharks. She kept talking to a big blond guy who looked a lot like Nathan Carter.

"It's the stingrays you should worry about, too," she said. "Very painful. And the jellyfish. Some jellyfish are so poisonous that they can kill a crocodile."

The man grunted. He didn't seem interested in all the deadly creatures of the sea. He was in good shape, with a crew cut. Maybe a Navy sailor.

The woman persisted. "But I worry about sharks the most because my uncle was eaten by one. In Australia."

For the rest of the trip in, Brian listened to her story about the unfortunate uncle. The blond guy watched the horizon and didn't comment. By the time they reached the pier, the sky had gone dark and the air smelled like bougainvillea. Christopher had already left a message that he'd gone ahead to one of the clubs and that Brian should meet him there.

"I need to go shower off," Brian said. "Do you want to come upstairs? Order something from room service?"

"No, I'm okay." Denny said. "You go ahead. I'll wait for you, walk you over."

In the shower, Brian worried that he'd pushed things too hard. Maybe Denny thought he'd meant they could shower together. Had Brian been that uncouth? He told himself to stop being silly. Still, it was a relief to find Denny waiting in the lobby downstairs. They walked toward the Priscilla Ann in mostly silence.

"You know what's over there?" Brian asked, desperate not to break the awkwardness. "Ernest Hemingway's old house."

Denny asked, "You like Hemingway?"

"Sure. Do you?"

"He's okay," Denny said. "Kind of sparse."

They detoured two blocks to the Hemingway House, a two-story white building lit up by floodlights amid all the greenery. "I don't think he was sparse," Brian said. "Economical. From the days when he was a journalist."

Denny leaned on the fence. "He drank too much and was bad to his wives."

"He had a disease. And lots of people are bad to their wives. Does that mean he wasn't a great writer?"

"No," Denny admitted. "It just means I don't have to like the guy."

Brian studied Denny's profile. The sweet air, the gentle breeze, and the seclusion of night made him want to lean over and kiss him. Before he could do anything that crazy stupid, Denny pushed back off the fence.

"I've got to head back to Fisher Key with my brother," he said.

"Sure." Brian looked away before Denny could see his disappointment. So much for big romantic fantasies. "Maybe I'll see you up there this week."

"Okay."

"I mean, I know you're not gay, but it's nice to have a friend." Brian hoped he didn't sound like a dork.

Denny looked surprised. "You have friends up there."

"Not so much. It's my own fault. I don't get out much."

"We'll get you out some more," Denny said, flashing that smile of his, and Brian hoped he meant it.

❖

Steven spent his afternoon bumming around the beach, watching girls, and drinking soda in different spots along Duval Street. He saw some military officers eating in an open-air restaurant and tried not to get jealous that they had careers, they had futures. He wandered over to watch a cruise ship pull out into the harbor and by the old Custom House he saw Eddie Ibarra and Lisa Horne walk by.

"Eddie!" Steven exclaimed.

Eddie stopped. He was wearing rumpled clothes and a Key West ball cap. Lisa was in a purple T-shirt and purple eye shadow and purple feather earrings. Who even wore feather earrings? She had two large shopping bags in her hands.

"Hey," Eddie said, glassy-eyed. "What are you doing here?"

"Karate, you douchebag. I've been calling you since yesterday. Where's your phone?"

"He lost it," Lisa said, nuzzling the side of Eddie's face. Her sunglasses slipped, showing her bloodshot eyes. "Didn't you, baby?"

"Completely lost," Eddie agreed. "What are you doing in town?"

"Karate," Steven repeated. "Are you stoned?"

"No!"

Steven was sure he was lying. "You're supposed to be in Miami."

"Change of plans," Lisa said.

She started to tug him away but stopped when Steven said, "The FBI is looking for you."

Eddie asked, "What?"

Lisa asked, "Why?"

"That bag you found at Beacon Point," Steven said. "They think it's a clue to whoever blew up that yacht. What was in it?"

"Nothing," Lisa said.

"Some clothes," Eddie said. "We threw them in the ocean."

"What kind of clothes?"

Lisa made a face. "Some stupid clothes. Who cares? It's not a clue to anything."

"Just clothes." Eddie held up his hand in an oath. "In the ocean. I swear."

Lisa said, "We've got to go."

She pulled Eddie away. He went with her, docile, but called over his shoulder, "We're at the Pier House! Come by later."

Steven said nothing. A year ago he and Eddie had been best of friends, living practically in each other's pockets. Nothing and nobody came between them—not booze or pot or a girl tagged Most Likely To Overdose.

Now he seemed like a total stranger.

As they walked away, Lisa threw a backward glance over her shoulder that said Steven wasn't welcome to drop by later. Or ever.

But Steven had already figured that out.

"The Pier House?" Denny asked on the drive home. "Where'd they get that kind of money?"

Steven didn't answer. The Overseas Highway was full of dark stretches, and he was keeping a close eye out for key deer. The little animals could dart out into the road at any minute. The smell of the ocean rolled through the open windows, salty and heavy.

"Why are you giving me the silent treatment?"

"I'm not."

"Then answer me."

"I don't know where they got the money. Maybe Lisa's grandmother gave it to them."

"The one who thinks they went to Miami?"

"It's none of our business."

Denny snorted. "Since when is anything not our business?"

"Since we graduated and we know better."

Another bridge rolled by underneath them. Steven's fingers ached from holding the steering wheel so tightly. His stomach twisted the same way it had back at graduation.

"Things change," he said. "Everyone's leaving in August or September, and nothing will be like it used to be."

"Are you moping over Eddie?" Denny asked. "Is this a bromance thing?"

"Do you want me to drive into the ocean and drown you?"

"You wouldn't drive into the ocean. You like your truck too much." Denny slurped the last of the cherry drink he'd picked up at the gas station. "Just relax and enjoy the summer, will you? Stop worrying about what's going to change in the fall."

"I didn't get in," Steven said. He instantly bit his tongue. He hadn't meant to blurt it out. But there it was: the plain, ridiculous truth. And his heart was rat-tatting with nervousness now that Denny knew, but he was glad he'd said it.

"Didn't get what?" Denny asked.

"What?"

"Didn't get it. Get what?"

Denny had misheard. Because his brain was full of would-be gay boyfriend, probably.

"Nothing."

"Nothing what?"

"You're deaf, do you know that?" Steven said. "Just forget it."

Denny turned on the radio. "Call me when you're ready to stop being so irritating."

"Likewise."

They rode the rest of the way in silence.

CHAPTER SEVENTEEN

On Monday morning Denny woke to see Steven hunched over in the pre-dawn light, tying his sneakers.

"I'll go with you," Denny croaked out. He needed a good run.

"Don't slow me down," Steven warned him.

The morning breeze promised a hot, steamy day to come. They ran their normal four-mile loop on back roads, crossing the Overseas Highway to get to the long stretch that passed the resorts, police station, baseball field, and private homes. Steven didn't set a particularly fast pace, which was a surprise. Usually he pushed and pushed until Denny's legs felt rubbery. They heard birds, the occasional passing of cars, and their own labored breathing.

The last part of the route took them past Beacon Point, the yacht club, and the city marina. Once home, they threw themselves into the lagoon and swam out to the channel markers. Denny liked the feel of water sluicing over his shoulders and legs. Usually Steven was faster, but today he lagged behind. They returned and hauled themselves up to the dock. Usually they did push-ups then, but Steven just flopped on his back. No noise came from inside the house. Mom and Dad were still asleep.

"What didn't you get?" Denny asked curiously.

"What?"

"Last night. What didn't you get?"

Steven made a face. "Will you drop it?"

"No. Tell me."

Steven pulled himself upright and walked away. Denny thought about giving him some space, but then followed him down the dirt drive toward the main road.

"I didn't get in," Steven finally said. "Happy?"

"What are you talking about? In what?"

Steven threw his hands up. "BUD/S! SEAL training. Any of it!"

Denny stopped walking.

"That's crazy," he said. "You showed the papers to Mom and Dad."

"They're fake. Eddie did them on the library computer."

Denny felt the whole island shift under his feet—the big oak trees and palm trees warping in his vision, the ocean threatening to sweep over his head.

"You faked it? And the only one who knew was Eddie Ibarra?"

"Yes. Aren't you happy you asked?" Steven put his hands on his knees. His voice dropped, as if he were deflating. "I didn't get in."

Denny walked a loop around him. "But that's insane. Why not? What's wrong with you?"

"I failed the color vision test."

"The what?"

"I'm color-blind!"

Denny burst out laughing. He didn't mean to, honest, but *color-blind*?

Steven looked ready to punch him. "I'm glad you think it's funny."

A truck turned out of the city marina and came their way. They separated to let it pass.

"What color was that?" Denny asked, once it was gone.

"Blue."

"So how can you be color-blind?"

Steven threw his hands up in the air. "The military has a different test. It's harder than the normal test. They won't let you be a SEAL if you can't pass it, and I didn't want to train for anything else. So I'm not in."

Denny had never heard Steven sound so defeated. Sure, he'd had temporary setbacks—a broken leg during freshman year, getting the flu before the SATs. Nothing like this.

"I'll take it for you," Denny announced. "They won't be able to tell the difference. I'm not afraid of any stupid machine."

It wouldn't be the first time they'd swapped identities without telling anyone, but Steven shook his head.

"You can't. If I'm really color blind, I could get people killed on a mission. I have no business doing the job."

Steven started walking back home. Denny followed silently. Being a SEAL was all that Steven had ever wanted. He'd planned for it, dreamed of it.

"So what are you going to do?"

"I don't know." Steven swung around. "You can't tell Mom or Dad."

"You don't think they'll notice when you never leave for boot camp?"

"I'll have a plan by then."

"College."

"It's too late for the fall term."

"Community college, so you can transfer the credit."

"I'm not going to community college."

Denny thought fast. "You could join the Army. They have divers."

"I'm not joining the Army, asstard," Steven said. "Don't worry about it, okay? I'll figure something out. You just keep your mouth shut."

Musing about it later, as he biked the half-mile to Mom's bookstore, Denny figured that Steven had told him because he wanted help. He simply couldn't admit it, because he was a big macho jerk. But what kind of help could Denny offer? He was still thinking about it when he parked his bike against the back concrete wall of the Florida Keys Bookmine.

No other store from Miami to Key West could match Mom's store. She had bought it from an old-timer who'd built every shelf himself and had little interest in alphabetizing, organizing, or making the aisles navigable. As a little kid Denny had gotten lost more than once in the towering stacks of books, overwhelmed by the smell of musty old paper and yellowed light bulbs.

Now, ten years later, the store had clear diagrams for shopping, shelves that were actually labeled, and two annexes for the overflow of books. Two steps inside reminded Denny how nice it was to have air-conditioning, too. Three steps inside, he was ambushed by Sean Garrity and Robin McGee.

Sean's hair was sticking up in more directions than usual, his eyebrows drawn together in consternation. "You nearly die, you get saved by some random Adonis, and then you take off for the weekend without telling every dirty detail to your best friends! What's wrong with that?"

Denny felt contrite. "Sorry. I lost my phone. But it's not as exciting as you think."

"I hope it's more," Robin said as she and Sean trailed Denny toward the front desk. Her T-shirt today said, "I SUPPORT CIVIL RIGHTS" and she was wearing men's shorts. "We live vicariously through you. Don't you know that?"

"We want dirt," Sean said. "Moist, fertilized dirt."

"I don't even know what that means," Denny said.

"And we want to know about fireworks with Brian Vandermark," Robin said. "You and him in a boat? Mouth-to-mouth CPR?"

Denny spun around and brought both of them to a halt. Through the shelves he could see his mother making a sale to two tourists in fishing hats.

"No fireworks!" he told them, low but vehement. "None! Nothing. You know I'm not interested in that."

They gazed at him in frank disbelief.

"For years you've been denying it," Sean said, with an eye roll.

"We're not fooled," Robin added.

"Nothing," Denny repeated. "And if you say anything in front of my mom I'll have to kill both of you in the most unpleasant way possible."

He didn't mean to sound so snippish, or maybe he did, because at least they didn't follow him to the register.

Mom said, "Hcy, here you are," as if she hadn't seen him at breakfast just a half hour ago. Her gaze immediately narrowed. "What's wrong?"

"Nothing," he said.

She peered up at him, short but stubborn. Her dress today was yellow with orange palm trees on it. His eyes watered if he looked too long at it.

"No lying, Dennis Andrew," she said.

The truth was impossible, though. How could he tell her he was a closet homosexual in lust with both the rich Brian Vandermark and the much older Nathan Carter? Or that Steven was lying about the military and the SEALs?

"I'm just tired, Mom. Steven snored all night. Give me some iced coffee and I'm all set."

She tapped the end of his nose. "All right. Coming right up."

The store wasn't too busy. Denny switched the radio on, tuning it to an oldies station out of Miami. The customers liked it, even if it made him think he was stuck in a Clark Gable movie. Sean and Robin had been assigned to shelving books in the Romance section, and he could hear them mocking the cover pictures of lovers, bosoms, and bare chests.

An hour after the store opened, Dad came in with two men in suits. One of the men was retirement age, with thin white hair and an ill-fitting suit. The other was much younger, Hispanic, and had very expensive shoes.

Denny recognized him immediately—the man in Key West who'd warned them about asking questions about Nathan Carter.

"This is Agent Garcia and Agent Crown of the Miami FBI office." Dad adjusted his gun belt. "They want to talk to you, Dennis."

CHAPTER EIGHTEEN

Steven went to work feeling strange. It was a relief to finally have told Denny the truth. But at the same time saying the words aloud made the whole thing more real. He really had been turned down. He wasn't going to be a SEAL.

Because of some stupid defect in his eyes.

Color-blind. It was ridiculous.

He put his keys and cell phone in his locker, punched in, and went outside to the beautifully landscaped garden. About a half dozen guests were already in the pool, which was open before and after the lifeguard was on duty. Steven scooped up crystal blue water in vials for the mandatory chemical test, noted the perfectly fine results on his clipboard, and climbed up into his chair overlooking the deep end.

A half hour later, Kelsey Carlson and Jennifer O'Malley showed up. Kelsey's dad did legal work for the resort and was comped free admission to the pool all year long.

"How was Key West?" Kelsey asked, as if he hadn't answered every one of her messages all weekend. She knew he'd gone to class, and knew he'd gone out on a WaveRunner, and knew that he'd run into Eddie.

He hadn't told her about Bethany. A guy had to have a little breathing room, after all.

"Good," he said and came down from his chair for a kiss. "Hi, Jen."

Jennifer flashed him a brilliant white smile. She was wearing a tiny blue bikini with white dots on it. The top of it barely held in her breasts, which were much bigger than they'd been last summer. She was always showing off her latest fashion purchases online, and he was pretty sure he recognized the designer beach bag she'd brought along.

Not that he watched her webcasts.

Much.

"I heard you have a new mystery," Jen said. "Some boat blowing up?"

"Something like that," he said.

Kelsey stretched out on a chaise lounge in her own red bikini. Steven climbed back into his chair and tried not to look too much at them—Kelsey all tall and lithe, Jennifer with her curves and glossy dark hair. Every now and then they whispered or giggled or sent him smiles. He wouldn't call himself paranoid, but he suspected they were comparing notes about him.

Just before lunchtime, Kelsey's phone rang.

"It's your brother, looking for you," she said. "He says it's important."

Steven took the call away from the pool deck, careful to keep an eye on the swimmers. "What?"

"The FBI's on their way to talk to you about *The Tempest*," Denny said. "They just left here. And you know one of them."

"I do?"

Thanks to Denny's forewarning, Steven wasn't surprised to meet Agent Garcia when Dad arrived. The FBI interviewed him in his manager's office, just off the gym where guests were using treadmills and lifting weights.

"I didn't see the boat explode," he said.

Agent Crown peered down his glasses at his notes. "They were with Mr. Nathan Carter."

Garcia didn't blink at Carter's name.

"Yes," Steven said.

"Your brother and Brian Vandermark are…friends?" Crown asked, his voice inflected at the end.

Dad didn't move from his position by the wall. He had his professional face on. You'd think he was disinterested, but he was really taking in every word.

"We all graduated together."

"Do you know why they were out on the water together?" Crown continued.

"You'd have to ask them," Steven said, trying not to get annoyed. He didn't like what Crown was insinuating. He especially didn't like that he was insinuating in front of Dad. Steven slid Garcia a glance. "I'm surprised you guys didn't come down Friday to ask all this."

"We only got assigned the case this morning," Garcia said stiffly.

"What about the agent who interviewed Brian Vandermark on Saturday night?" Steven asked.

Garcia and Crown exchanged looks.

Dad shifted his weight from one foot to the other.

"Which agent?" Garcia asked.

"Brian said some guy with a badge showed up and asked questions."

"We'll talk to our boss," Crown said. "Probably a mix-up."

Garcia didn't look so convinced.

The FBI agents left a few minutes later. Steven thought it was interesting that they didn't ask about Nathan Carter at all. He went back on duty at the pool and saw that Kelsey and Jennifer had both stretched out facedown on their lounges and undone the straps of their bikini tops.

"Will you put lotion on my back?" Kelsey asked sweetly.

"And mine," Jennifer added. "I don't want to burn."

The coconut-smelling lotion made his hands slippery. Kelsey's back was strong and broad, freckled in the sunlight. Jennifer's shoulders were smaller but more toned. When he looked at Kelsey he heard her saying, "It was a little fast." When he touched Jennifer, he remembered how they'd had sex in her big white bed while her parents were away. She'd never complained, not once, about his technique or style or speed.

At one o'clock, Kelsey starting packing up her things. "I have a hair appointment," she said. "Dinner tonight?"

"Sure," Steven said.

She kissed him. "Coming, Jen?"

Jennifer stretched out her legs. "No. I need more Vitamin D."

Steven got off his shift at three and ducked inside the locker room for a quick shower. Jennifer was waiting for him in the air-conditioned hallway when he was done. She'd pulled a low-cut white sundress over her bathing suit and freshened her lips with coral-colored lip gloss.

"I missed you at my party last week," she said.

Steven leaned against the wall. "Did you?"

Her perfectly tanned shoulder came to rest on the wall beside him as she leaned, too. "I shouldn't tell you," she said, with wide-eyed sincerity, "but Kelsey's been complaining about…you know. Your night together."

He kept his face blank. "What did she say?"

She shrugged. "She's got all the wrong ideas. Too many crazy books. I told her you were the best guy I'd done it with, and she should just learn to relax."

Steven studied her perfectly plucked eyebrows and smooth complexion. "Best guy, huh?"

Her smile was full of straight white teeth. "And I would do it again."

He couldn't deny that he was tempted. Couldn't pretend he hadn't spent all day acutely aware of her glossy hair and surgery-enhanced breasts.

"My parents aren't home," Jennifer said. "You should come over."

"And what would I tell Kelsey?"

Jennifer moved in closer. "Anything you want to."

Steven felt himself teetering.

"Have you ever read the *Kama Sutra*?" he asked.

"Never heard of it," she murmured, her mouth hot against his.

CHAPTER NINETEEN

Denny got off work at four. He biked over to the marina, but Nathan Carter wasn't aboard his boat.

"Walked himself over to the yacht club," Miss Nellie said from her folding chair.

A tourist with strawberry-blond hair and a floppy white hat was standing by the wreckage of *The Tempest*. Yellow police tape still surrounded the boat, but there was no sign of a guard. The strong breeze kept trying to push off the woman's hat and raise her red skirt up to her hips, which meant she was clutching her clothes while trying to talk into a tiny voice recorder.

"—you stop to think why anyone would destroy such a fine boat—" she was saying, and then the wind lifted her hat away completely.

"I'll get it," Denny volunteered.

He chased it down the dock for her. Clattering high heels sounded on the wood behind him. When he grabbed the hat and turned around, the woman was just a few feet behind—pretty, green-eyed, maybe twenty-two or twenty-three years old.

"Thanks!" she said, and jammed the hat back on top of her wild curls. "I only brought one hat. That's what you get when you jump into the car only half-packed and forget even to feed the fish. How long do you think goldfish last without food?"

"A day or two, maybe," he guessed.

Her smile widened. "Can I quote you on that? Are you a fish expert?"

"Mostly I catch and eat them. But I had an iguana once."

"You're an expert in my book." She stuck out her hand. "I'm Lucy Mcdaniel. What do you think of that yacht blowing up?"

Denny shook her hand. "I think whoever would destroy a ship like that ought to be keelhauled."

"I like that!" Lucy reached for her voice recorder. "I'll have to quote you for sure, now. I'm doing an article for *Florida Sail Magazine*."

"They sent someone down already?"

"Well, first I have to write it, then I have to try and sell it to them," Lucy said. "That's what I do. Freelance writing by day, underpaid and overworked waitress by night."

Denny liked her. She talked fast, like someone from New York, but she was the kind of girl he'd like to date if it weren't for being gay and everything. It was easier to talk to girls. Nothing was at stake.

"Good luck with the article," he said. "I'll read it when it gets published."

"Thanks. I hope they find the arsonist. I'll be watching with you when they keelhaul him."

Denny biked over to the yacht club next. The dining room and function rooms were closed, but the lounge was open to some yachtsmen drinking by the sunlit windows.

"Come on, Steven," said the bartender. "You know you're too young to be in here."

Denny didn't bother correcting him. "I'm looking for Nathan Carter. Big guy, blond—"

"Downstairs in the game room."

Nathan Carter was shooting pool by himself while a TV played softly in the corner. He was taller than Denny remembered, but also more handsome. Like a movie star who'd happened to drop by Fisher Key on his way to making a mega-blockbuster action flick. A gay movie star, according to Sensei Mike.

Carter sank two balls into a corner pocket before acknowledging Denny's presence. "How you feeling, kid? Cough up all that water yet?"

He sounded nice about it, like he genuinely cared. Which launched a whole new set of fantasies in Denny's brain.

"I'm okay. Thanks for saving my life."

Carter sank another ball. Nothing showy about it, just a man doing a job.

"You've got a funny way of showing gratitude," he said mildly. "Asking about me all over Key West?"

Busted.

Denny said, "You made us curious."

"If you're going to make discreet inquiries, the key part is 'discreet,'" Carter said. "I had four people send me messages. You ever hear the phrase 'Elephant in a china shop?'"

"I thought it was bull."

Carter raised an eyebrow.

"In a china shop," Denny said quickly. "Besides, no one talked. And your friend was pretty clear that we stop."

"Which friend?"

"Agent Garcia."

Carter reached for the pool chalk. He was wearing a white polo shirt and khaki pants, all of which showed off his physique very well. "We're not friends."

"That's not what he told us," Denny said.

A pause, then Carter bent over the table. "What else did he say?"

"Nothing. But he didn't sound like he was lying. Did the FBI come talk to you today? They talked to me."

Carter's next shot missed.

"I'm busy today. They're coming tomorrow." He straightened. "Why'd you come over here today?"

"Are you gay?"

Carter stared at him.

Denny wished he could surgically seal shut his own mouth. What kind of dumb question was that to blurt out? Especially to someone who'd probably studied torture in the military.

"You don't have to answer, but some people—it's not that it matters, but people think it about me sometimes, and they're wrong, and they should mind their own business, right?"

Carter was still staring at him. "Are you going to hyperventilate on me?"

"No," Denny said.

"Yes."

"Yes, I'm going to hyperventilate?"

"Yes, I'm gay," Carter said. "Anything else you want to know?"

Denny had about a thousand questions he could ask, but there was really only one he'd come to ask.

"I have a friend who wants to join the SEALs, but he got turned down because of some stupid color-blind test. Is there any way he could get around it?"

Carter started gathering the balls and lining them up in a black plastic triangle. "Would this friend happen to be your brother?"

"No!" Denny said. "He'd kill me if I told anyone."

"So it is your brother."

"Can we just remain anonymous?"

Carter took a pool stick off the wall and offered it to him. "How about this? Win a game, just one game, and we'll talk."

Talk over a candlelit table in some fancy restaurant? Talk while entwined in a big bed, satin sheets twisted around them? Denny's mind immediately detoured down a list of dirty possibilities.

"Well?" Carter asked.

Denny took the pool stick. "Ten bucks says I win."

Carter smiled widely. "You're on, kid."

CHAPTER TWENTY

Kelsey plucked one of Steven's onion rings from his plate. "Are you going to miss this?"

"Miss you stealing my food?"

"This place," she said. "Everything."

They were sitting in a corner booth at the L'il Conch Cafe, music and TVs blaring overhead for the tourist crowd. For a Monday night, the place was pretty crowded—a family of six at one big table, some old folks in the booth behind Kelsey, a pair of honeymooners feeding each other pasta and slices of garlic bread. Steven thought that was kind of sappy. The sun had gone down in a blaze of pink, and now the highway outside was dark and empty.

"Sure I'll miss it," he said. "You?"

"Miami's right next door. I'll be home every weekend."

He offered her another onion ring. It didn't make him feel less guilty. He wanted to say, "Hey, sorry about what happened today with me and your best friend," but telling her wouldn't do anything good, right? Besides, she looked great and was in a good mood and he didn't want to ruin anything

"But you're going to be all over the world," Kelsey continued. "You'll probably hardly ever get back here."

"I will when I can." That was part of the charade, that he'd get to leave like everyone else. That he wasn't digging a hole deeper for himself with every lie.

Kelsey tilted her head. "You're not eating much. Not hungry?"

"Guess not."

A pretty woman in jeans and a green shirt came up to their booth and started talking to Steven as if she knew him.

"So! Fish expert, iguana owner, and you know what keelhauling is, but you didn't tell me you nearly got killed when *The Tempest* blew up."

"What?" Steven asked.

Kelsey straightened on her seat. "Who's this?"

"I'm Lucy," she said. "And I'm pleased to meet you formally, Dennis Anderson."

"I'm Steven," he said.

Lucy's eyes widened. "Oh! The twin. Sorry. They said you were identical. Can I sit down?"

"No," Kelsey said. "We're having a private conversation."

He'd never seen her jealous like that. It was kind of nice.

"It'll only take a minute, promise." Lucy dragged a chair over and sat. She barely glanced at Kelsey. "I'm doing an article. Did you know the yacht was stolen in France a few years ago? No one's seen it since. But if you're going to steal a famous, million-dollar yacht, why sail it to Fisher Key and blow it up?"

"How famous?"

"As famous as Noah's Ark, if you run in certain circles." Lucy eyed Steven's onion rings as if contemplating stealing one. "Usually, if you burn something down or blow it up, you're trying to cover up a crime. But I talked to the local cops—that includes your dad—and no one found a corpse or anything interesting on what's left of the boat."

"Maybe it was revenge," Kelsey said.

Lucy finally noticed her. "Yes! But against who? The last owners were some private couple in Denmark. They only had it a year or two after buying it from some corporate bigwig."

Steven asked, "How many articles have you written?"

"I'm trying to break in," Lucy confided. "I'll write anything that'll put money in the bank. Last month I was in the *Orlando Times*. Just the op-ed pages. Okay, letters to the editor. Under a pseudonym.

But I graduated two years ago with a degree in journalism and you know what that gets you? Not a lot."

She talked too fast, Steven decided. He didn't trust people who talked that fast.

"Good luck with it," he said and pulled out his wallet.

"You can't leave! I need to ask you about what you saw that night."

"Ask Denny. He's not hard to find. Looks just like me."

Out in the truck, Kelsey said, "You were kind of rude."

"Reporters make me nervous."

She leaned across the bench seat and snuggled into his side. She smelled like some kind of floral perfume, light and airy. "If it'll make you feel any better, I have the keys to my dad's boat."

And because it was expected of him, because he couldn't really see any way out of it, and because he was eighteen years old, he said, "Okay."

When they were below decks, clothes off, the boat rocking beneath them, he made his very best effort to slow down and pay attention. But his stupid brain wouldn't stop comparing Kelsey and Jennifer. How Jennifer's body was smoother, and her waist smaller, and the noise she'd made when he sucked behind her ear—

"Ow," Kelsey said.

Steven lifted himself up. "What?"

"You're going to give me a hickey."

"That's the idea," he said.

"Don't." She kissed his fingers. "My dad will see it."

After they were done she wanted to cuddle in the small bunk. He ended up with his arm jammed against the bulkhead. She was heavy and warm against him, not saying much. He was sure she had more criticisms and was waiting to tell him every one.

"You okay?" she asked.

"Hungry like you wouldn't believe."

She laughed. "There's still food in the fridge."

He was scooping peanut butter out of a jar with a spoon when Eddie sent him a message: *Come on by, tequila party.* When he went back to the cabin, Kelsey was pulling on her blouse.

"What's wrong?" he asked.

"Nothing. My dad and I are supposed to go to Miami in the morning. I better get home." Kelsey pulled back her hair and then leaned forward to give him a long, wet kiss. "But that was a lot better than last time."

She said it like a teacher giving him a star on his book report.

Steven said, "I aim to please, ma'am."

"Maybe next time you don't have to be so loud," she suggested.

The funny thing about that? Jennifer hadn't complained one bit.

CHAPTER TWENTY-ONE

How did the FBI do today?" Denny asked Dad, passing over a container of egg foo yong. Mom was at a Chamber of Commerce banquet. Steven had gone straight from work to having dinner with Kelsey. Afterward, Steven and Kelsey were probably going to have sex. Not that Denny was jealous.

"Six interviews, and I don't think they found out anything useful," Dad said. "The only break they're going to get is if forensics turns up something off that boat, or if they find the mystery swimmer."

"What are the chances?" Denny asked.

"Not so good." Dad shuffled some cartons of rice and spare ribs on the table. "Why didn't you mention that other FBI agent before? The one in Key West?"

"Oh," Denny said. "I guess I forgot."

Dad gave him a patient look.

Denny flushed. "You always say don't volunteer everything when it comes to dealing with the feds."

"What about volunteering everything when it comes to dear old dad?"

Trust me, Dad, Denny almost said. You don't want to know everything that goes through my head. Like how blue Brian's eyes were behind a swim mask, or how Nathan Carter's muscles moved when he took a pool shot, or any of the eleven dirty fantasies Denny regularly enjoyed in the shower.

"I appreciate that you boys like to solve mysteries on your own," Dad continued. "But I expect to be told everything. You understand?"

"Yes, Dad."

"Any other secrets you need to get off your chest?"

That was it—his opening. His chance to come clean. "Dad, I'm gay" was all he had to say, and Dad would be surprised but cool about it, and they'd never talk about it again.

"Nope," Denny said. "No other secrets."

"Good. Pass the wontons."

They ate Chinese food until they were stuffed. Denny was cleaning up the kitchen when Brian texted him: *Want 2 come over hang out?*

He hesitated over his response. Sure he wanted to. But what if he went over and did something stupid that he couldn't take back? Or that Brian misinterpreted friendship for romance? This whole burgeoning friendship thing could be over in an instant.

"Who's that?" Dad asked.

"Just someone from school," Denny said.

"A girl someone?"

"Dad."

Dad grinned. "Just asking."

He rode his bike over with the sun low in the west and insects droning in the mangroves. The Vandermarks lived in the second-most expensive home on the island, with its Spanish tile roof and circular driveway and separate two-car garage. The windows reflected the Atlantic waters. Though there was a private dock, no boat was moored at it. Brian answered the front door wearing a Key West T-shirt, loose and clean.

"Christopher's still around," he warned. "We were about to leave for the Miami airport when the FBI showed up. He missed his flight and he's in a bad mood."

"Got it," Denny said.

The inside of the house had high ceilings, immaculate tile floors, and an open floor plan. The furniture in the enormous living room/dining room was all white or glass or metal. The kitchen area was full of stainless steel. Eddie Ibarra's mom, Caroline, was finishing up some dishes in the sink. He knew that she cooked and cleaned for some families on the island, but not that she worked for the Vandermarks.

"Hello, Steven," she said.

"Hi, Mrs. Ibarra. I'm Denny."

"Of course you are." She was thin and gray-haired, always somber. "Sorry."

A younger, much prettier woman emerged from a hallway. She was wearing white yoga pants and a bright yellow top. Sort of the hippie granola type, Denny decided, even if the rest of the house looked like it belonged to the rich and famous.

"I'm Hannah," she said. "I didn't get to meet you the other night, with all that confusion, but Brian speaks very well of you."

"Mom," Brian groaned.

"I'm only repeating you," Mrs. Vandermark said. "Would you boys like any organic strawberries?"

"Thanks, but I just ate," Denny said.

Mrs. Ibarra folded up her dish towel. "I've got to be going. Tomorrow's okay?"

"Yes, thank you," Mrs. Vandermark said. "Here, take some of this fruit home. I bought too much."

Mrs. Ibarra looked faintly embarrassed, but she took the fruit. As Denny trailed Brian toward the other side of the house he said, "Did you know that's Eddie's mom?"

"No." Brian sounded surprised. "I never made the connection."

Brian's room was about three times the size of Denny's, with dark furniture, a padded leather headboard on the bed, and bookcases that took up one entire wall. The cherry desk and computer near the windows probably cost more than Denny made all summer working for his mother.

"Make yourself at home," Brian said, switching on a wall-mounted flat-screen TV. "I've got six or seven games from Christmas that I never opened, if you're interested."

Denny was busy inspecting Brian's bookcases. At least a hundred different hardcovers filled the shelves, and not the cheap ones either. Hawthorne, Twain, Hemingway, Grisham. Male authors, every one of them.

"Did you read all these or are they just for show?" Denny asked.

"Who would I show?" Brian said. "I read every one."

"Who's your favorite?"

Brian inspected the books alongside Denny. "Twain, I guess. You can't beat a boy and runaway slave on a raft down the Mississippi."

"I like *Tom Sawyer* better. The cave, the gang, the robbers—good stuff."

Brian smiled fondly at him. "I should have known. Tom Sawyer solved mysteries, too."

That smile made Denny nervous. He moved away quickly and plopped into the leather swivel chair in front of the computer. "How'd the FBI thing go?"

"They asked a lot of questions about the agent at the Casa Marina," he said. "What he asked, what he said. I wasn't sure about whether to tell them about our room being robbed, but Christopher sure told them."

"How'd your parents take it?"

"They're freaking out in their own unique ways. Henrik's locked himself in his study and Mom's been doing yoga for hours." Brian gazed blankly at the TV screen, where a commercial for beer was playing. "I guess I'm kind of weirded out, too. I'm glad you came over."

"Any time," Denny said. "Where are those games?"

He wasn't much into first-person shooter games, but one of the titles, *Secrets of Organon*, was some kind of adventure about minotaurs kidnapping Aristotle in ancient Greece. Historical accuracy was not its strong point. They plugged it in, picked avatars, and poked around Athens a few minutes before Mrs. Vandermark poked her head in.

"How about some ice cream, boys? We have hot fudge sundae, caramel sauce, imported nuts—"

"Mom," Brian complained. "We can find the refrigerator if we need to."

She smiled uncertainly. When she was gone, Brian confessed, "She has the wrong idea about you."

"What idea is that?"

Brian blushed a little. "That I'm only interested in your body."

Denny's stomach flipped.

"I told her it's not that way," Brian said hastily. "Promise."

Denny concentrated on the screen. "How long have they known about you?"

"My mom figured it out in fifth grade. I had a big goofy crush on my soccer coach. All season I'd follow him up and down the field. Must have driven him nuts. From then on she started buying books about gay daddies and lesbian mommies and, well, I could always talk to her after that."

"And your dad?"

"My birth dad disappeared when I was a kid." Brian turned his remote control in time to avoid being pummeled by a minotaur. "Henrik's okay about it. He's pretty okay about everything, usually. Except lately. Since *The Tempest* blew up. The FBI agents made him even more jumpy."

"Does he have anything to hide?"

"What, like a white-collar criminal?" Brian shook his head. "He made his fortune in jewelry. Since coming to America it's all been investments. He's a day trader, all sorts of stocks."

"Hey, Brian, I need to borrow—" Christopher said, walking into the room without knocking. He was damp from the shower, wearing only a fluffy white towel around his hips. He looked at Denny and Brian sitting on the end of the bed and said, snidely, "Am I interrupting?"

Denny turned back to the TV without comment. Brian said, "No, you're not interrupting. What do you need to borrow?"

"A clean shirt. Your mom's washing all of mine."

Brian flipped on the lights to a walk-in closet. Christopher followed him into it. Denny tried not to watch. Christopher was ridiculously handsome, with well-defined muscles and acres of smooth skin.

"You're not going out all night, are you?" Brian asked, picking out some shirts on hangers. "We have to leave at seven tomorrow morning to make your new flight."

"I'll be home early, Mom," Christopher said sarcastically. "I'm just going to that girl Lisa's house to have some fun. You know, fun? Not a four-letter word."

"Smoking pot's not my idea of fun," Brian said.

But this is, Denny thought victoriously. *Staying here with me.*

"There's a clinical diagnosis for what you have," Christopher said. "It's called stick-in-the-mud. When you come back to Boston, we're going to have to cure it for you."

Oh, yeah. Denny understood that dig.

"Remember," Brian said. "We leave at seven."

After Christopher left, Brian sat on the bed and looked glum. "I guess I'm not a very good host."

Denny said, "I know what could make you a better one."

"What's that?"

"Ice cream. With hot fudge sauce and maybe some caramel and what else did your mom say? Imported nuts."

Brian smiled. "We can do that."

CHAPTER TWENTY-TWO

S teven took Kelsey home, kissed her good night, and drove over to Eddie's. The Ibarras lived in a concrete block house with a carport full of junk. Eddie's Hyundai was parked in the weedy grass, but his mom's old Civic was gone. Other cars were parked along a fence that was falling off its posts.

The front door was open, spilling light and movie noise through a torn screen door. Steven knocked.

"Yeah, come in," Eddie called out.

Eddie was on his sofa next to two guys from school—Paul Leroy and Joshua Garrity, Sean's younger brother. Two bottles of tequila sat opened on the coffee table beside some beer cans and red plastic cups. Paul and Joshua were smoking cigarettes.

Paul raised a hand.

"Hey," Joshua said.

"It's a drinking game," Eddie said as some mindless action movie blazed across what looked like a new TV. "Sit down."

The house was hot and smelled like bad laundry. Steven said, "Can I talk to you outside?"

"What? You mad at me?" Eddie asked.

"It's about the FBI."

Eddie grimaced. "Okay, whatever."

Steven led him out into the yard. Before everything went bad with the booze, Eddie's father had put up a homemade swing set. The metal had long since rusted, but the seats were mostly intact.

You could swing without worrying too much that the whole thing would fall over.

"Where'd you get the new TV?" Steven asked.

"Graduation gift," Eddie said, sitting on one of the seats. He wouldn't look Steven in the eye. "What's it to you?"

"You go to Key West and stay at the Pier House," Steven said steadily. "Now you've got a new TV and surround stereo sound. No one's giving you that stuff as a graduation gift."

"They could," Eddie protested. "You don't know."

"You partied all weekend and wouldn't answer your phone—"

"I told you that I lost it."

"You must have found it again," Steven said. "You called me from your regular number."

"Why are you treating me like a criminal?" Eddie asked angrily. "I didn't do anything wrong but find the money."

From the house came the sounds of explosions and screams. Paul laughed. Or maybe that was Joshua.

"What money?" Steven asked.

Eddie grabbed the chains of his swing and leaned back, his gaze toward the sky. Cloudy night, no sign of the crescent moon. Steven couldn't hear the ocean over the sound of the TV.

"There was some money in the bag," he said, sounding tired. "Finders keepers, right? There was no wallet or ID."

Steven wanted to knock him flat in the scrub grass and shake some sense into him.

"How much?"

"Why do you have to be so annoying about it?"

"Because whoever it belongs to might be tied to the boat that blew up, you idiot. What if they want it back?" Steven asked.

Eddie straightened. "It's not like that."

"It's not? How?"

"Because. It wasn't a lot. Just like, a thousand dollars. Maybe two thousand. Small change."

Steven was getting a headache. "You didn't report it to the police."

"Of course not! It's ours. Lisa and I found it. Nobody else even looked into the bag. So what if we threw the clothes and keys away?"

"What keys?"

"Some car keys. But there was no car. So the whole bag was probably just something that got lost. Not everything's got to be some criminal conspiracy you have to solve."

Steven didn't answer.

Eddie squeezed the bridge of his nose. "Maybe it's not a lot of money to you. But my mom deserves a new TV, and we filled her prescriptions, too. So what if we spent the rest? No one's going to come looking for it."

Except someone had, Steven thought. Someone had swiped Brian Vandermark's hotel room key and searched his room because Christopher had gone on TV and announced seeing the explosion from Beacon Point.

"You should have told the truth since the beginning," Steven said.

"Like you did?" Eddie asked. "Have you started packing for boot camp yet?"

Silence stretched between them, taut and unhappy.

"You don't know what it's like to be broke all the time," Eddie said. "You don't know what it's like to have none of the answers. What am I going to do in September? Community college. Which I'm probably going to fail out of. Maybe later I can get a job at the Dollar Mart. You don't have the SEALs but you've got options."

"I don't know what they are," Steven said.

"But you'll figure them out. You always do."

A shooting star crossed the sky. Steven wished he was on it, riding fire to the other side of the sky.

"Come inside and watch a movie," Eddie said. "I'll send those other guys home. We'll pretend it's ninth grade, first time we ever had beer."

"First time you ever had beer, you mean."

"Show off."

Steven shrugged. "Is it my fault I matured early?"

CHAPTER TWENTY-THREE

Denny returned from Brian's house to find Mom asleep and Dad sacked out in front of the TV watching a John Wayne movie. Dad liked John Wayne. Denny liked cowboys in tight jeans. When the credits rolled at midnight Dad said, "Call your brother and tell him he's about to be grounded."

Ten minutes later, Steven came home looking sheepish. "Sorry. I was at Eddie's and lost track of time."

Dad scrutinized him thoroughly. Denny knew he was looking for signs of being drunk or high. Sometimes Dad couldn't turn off being a cop.

"We were watching movies," Steven said, unflinching.

"And you missed curfew," Dad said. "What's your punishment?"

"I could be home an hour early tomorrow night," Steven offered.

"Or you could be home all tomorrow night," Dad said.

Steven didn't argue.

Behind the closed door of their room Denny said, "Were you really at Eddie's?"

Steven stripped off his shirt. "You don't believe me?"

"Sure I do. Did you find out how he could afford the Pier House?"

"There was money in that duffel bag." Steven plucked a T-shirt out of the pile next to his bed and sniffed it. "A couple thousand dollars in cash. They blew it all."

"Wow."

"And there were keys, too. Some kind of car keys. He says they threw them in the water."

"Maybe that's what the break-in was about in Key West."

"That's what I think." Steven flopped down on the bed. "I don't know what to do about him."

Denny sat on his own bed. "I've got some news. I talked to Nathan Carter."

"About what?"

"About SEAL training."

Steven gave him a narrow look. "What about it?"

"About the vision test."

Steven sat up, looking thunderous. "You told him?"

Denny backed away. Their bedroom didn't give him much maneuvering room. "He said anyone who fails the military vision test can get a waiver from the Director of Military Medicine."

Steven grabbed a pillow and stepped toward him. "You told him I got turned down?"

"Keep shouting and Mom and Dad will hear," Denny warned.

"I can kill you quietly."

"I told him it was someone I knew! Not you."

"You don't think he can figure it out?"

"And he said he's gay. But whatever went on with him and Agent Garcia, he's not saying."

Steven readied the pillow as if to shove it down Denny's throat. "I don't care about his love life. I tell you the most important thing in my life and you go blab it. Why don't you put it on a billboard on the highway?"

"When did you become King Melodrama?" Denny asked. "You're not listening. You could get a waiver."

Steven dropped the pillow and shook his head. "Yeah, because a piece of paper is going to save my team one day when we have to defuse a bomb and I can't tell the blue wire from the green wire."

"You're not color-blind. I don't know why you're giving up so quickly."

Steven flopped down on his mattress and threw an arm up over his eyes. "Stop talking about stuff you don't know anything about."

Denny wanted to strangle him. And he wanted to talk about Brian, and his books, and his bedroom overlooking the sea, and how it wasn't a date if you just hung out with a guy, right?

He threw himself into bed. It took a long, long time before he fell asleep.

❖

"I should drive you boys up to Miami," Henrik said just before Brian and Christopher were supposed to leave.

Brian was filling two travel mugs with some of Mom's fresh ground coffee. "No, it's okay. I'm just dropping him off and coming right back."

Henrik had dark circles under his eyes. Although he usually dressed nicely for a man who worked from home, today he was wearing jeans and a polo shirt with a small stain on the front. Henrik never wore anything with stains.

"It's no problem," Henrik said. "Maybe we could go shopping later. You'll need things for school."

"I figured I'd buy stuff when I'm there," Brian said.

Mom was watching them quietly from her stool. She was wrapped in a fluffy pink bathrobe he hadn't seen since the winter in Boston. "It's not a bad idea to let Henrik drive, honey. You had an exciting weekend."

Brian chafed under the concern. "Quit with the worrying, okay? I'm eighteen. Not twelve."

Christopher wandered out of his bedroom with a Boston Red Sox cap pulled low over his eyes. "Don't even tell me it's time to go."

Brian got him and his stuff piled into the Honda and kissed his mom good-bye. He half expected Henrik to follow them anyway. Sometimes he wished they'd be a little looser. A little less hovering.

"Wake me when we're there," Christopher muttered, slouching low in the passenger seat.

Brian turned the radio up loudly.

The first island after Fisher Key was Lower Matecumbe. Brian thought most of the Overseas Highway was boring—one flat key after the next, strips of modern concrete buildings interspersed with old tourist hotels, gas stations, and marine stores. Marshes and mangroves, lots of trees, lots of asphalt. The prettiest spots were off the highway, the best views from the long bridges spanning channels that connected the Gulf of Mexico and Straits of Florida.

Looking at the blue and green water—shimmering under the sun, the infinite seas—made him think of Denny and their snorkeling trip, and how he'd like to do it again.

They stopped for gas near Theater of the Sea, where you could pay to swim with dolphins. Christopher bought two glazed doughnuts and shared one.

"Did you have a nice time with your not-gay friend last night?" he asked when Brian was on the road again.

"You don't have to be like that."

"Being repressed doesn't make him less gay," Christopher observed. "Macho hero thing, I get it. But he wouldn't be clinging to you if he was straight."

"I can't have straight friends?"

"You can have dozens of them. He's just not one of them."

Traffic grew heavier as they passed through Plantation Key. Brian checked his gauges. The car felt sluggish. Like back up north, driving in winter snow—heavy and not as responsive as usual. He hoped he didn't need to get it serviced.

"If he is gay, which he's not, it's his business and not ours," Brian said. "Maybe he has good reasons for not telling anyone."

"Yeah, he's scared. In denial. Homophobic."

"You can't just go labeling people you don't know."

"Sure I can. I do it all the time."

The road had widened to two lanes, but would soon be narrowing again. A black Toyota was tailgating Brian. He hated people who tailgated. And he hated Christopher's casual indictment.

"If you had spent any time with him at all you'd know he's not like that," Brian said.

"I didn't spend any time with him because he was all over you, trying to get his tongue down your throat."

"Are you jealous?" Brian gaped at him. "Is that it?"

The black Toyota gunned past them. The tinted windows hid the driver. Maybe some hyperactive businessman late for a meeting in Miami.

"I am never jealous because I—" Christopher said.

Brian missed the rest of that sentence. He missed it because the Toyota had barely cleared him before swerving back into the narrowing northbound lane. Brian braked hard. The pedal locked and the car spun out.

"Stop!" Christopher yelled.

As if he had a choice.

They crashed hard into a railing right before the next bridge. It gave way in splinters of metal and wood, plummeting them down a short embankment into the sea below.

The long, frantic blast of the car horn filled the air.

Chapter Twenty-four

Denny and Steven ran four miles that morning, looping around the island shortly after dawn turned the sky gold. Steven set a breakneck pace to punish Denny for telling Nathan Carter about the vision test. Denny hung in there, though, never once complaining. Afterward they swam out to the channel marker, came back in, and sprawled at the end of the deck in the morning sunlight.

"You've got that stupid look on your face again," Steven warned.

"What look?"

"Thinking about your gay not-boyfriend look."

Denny scowled at him. "I thought you wanted me to hook up."

"I want you to do it or stop moping about it."

"I think you should concentrate on your own love life, Romeo."

Steven kicked up water with his dangling feet. Gulls flapped overhead, reflecting in the placid water.

Denny squinted at the sky. "Think about that duffel bag. Clothes can be replaced. Two thousand bucks isn't really that much. Maybe whoever broke into Brian's room at the Casa Marina was looking for the only other thing in that bag. The keys."

"For what? If you can blow up a boat, you can hotwire a car."

"Maybe Eddie was wrong. Maybe they weren't car keys at all, or there were more than just car keys on the ring. There could have been keys to a safe deposit box, or a home safe, or another boat."

"All of those can be replaced."

"If you have the time. But not if you're in a hurry, or you don't want to draw attention to yourself."

Steven snorted and kicked up more water. "You mean like impersonating an FBI agent? Whoever that Agent Prosper was, he interviewed Brian when he should have been interviewing Douchebag."

Denny stared at him. "What was his name?"

"Prosper."

"No."

"Yes."

"I can't believe I didn't see it."

"See what?"

Denny rushed up the dock to their house. The bookcase in their room needed some serious culling—too many beloved books from their childhood now forgotten—but he found what he was looking for.

Steven had followed him in. "What do you need Shakespeare for?"

Denny opened to the list of characters for *The Tempest* and pointed.

"Prospero, duke of Milan," Steven said. "So what? It's a coincidence."

"Is it?" Denny asked. "I think we better go over to Beacon Point and look for those keys."

"I'll get Dad's metal detector," Steven said.

It took forty minutes of searching with the underwater metal detector before Steven found a silver key ring buried in some silt.

"I win!" Steven immediately said.

"Win what?"

"Whatever I want."

Denny snatched the key ring away and dangled it in mid-air. Two matching car keys hung off the ring.

"Master key and valet key," Denny said.

Steven asked, "Mr. Personality said no cars were parked here Thursday night. You think he was lying?"

Denny scanned the parking lot, the tree line, and the road nearby.

"Or maybe it wasn't parked where they would notice it," he said. "Where does Dad's office tow all abandoned cars?"

Ten minutes later they were on the road north to Plantation Key. The impound lot was a few acres of dirt and grass located behind a chain fence with rusty NO TRESPASSING signs on it. The attendant was old Will Soames, who'd spent most of his life sponge diving until a crippling stroke. He looked like someone who'd spent most of his life underwater—pale, wrinkled fingers twisted up like pieces of driftwood.

"What kind of car you looking for?" Soames asked.

"We don't know," Denny said. "Something towed in since Friday morning."

Soames leaned back in his wobbly chair. The chair, his desk, and a battered filing cabinet were the only furniture in an office wallpapered with pinup calendars. A marine radio decorated one shelf, next to a police scanner and an old ham radio.

"You boys working a case for your dad?" Soames asked.

"Working a case," Steven agreed.

Denny added, "For a friend."

"I don't know, boys." Soames heaved a sigh. "If there's a car here, you're going to want into it. And if you get into it and there's some kind of trouble, I'm the one they're going to hang."

"There won't be any trouble," Denny promised.

"And we'll make it worth your while," Steven added.

Soames laced his hands over his belly and grinned toothlessly. "Let's discuss what that would take."

A few minutes later, after agreeing to take Soames out tarpon fishing on the day of his choice, Denny and Steven were standing in front of a silver Ford SUV, late model. From the outside it looked clean, with no suspicious smells emanating from it.

"Look here," Steven said, crouching next to the Florida license plate.

Denny saw a faint seam running down the middle of it. "Someone welded two different plates together."

"Bogus plate," Steven said.

The key opened the door. Careful not to leave any fingerprints, Steven searched under the seats and Denny checked the glove compartment. Only two items were inside.

"Payday," Denny said.

"What?" Steven asked.

"One portable computer hard drive," Denny said. "And one paperback copy of *The Tempest*."

Steven whistled in appreciation. "We were meant to find these."

"Someone was meant to find them," Denny agreed. "I wonder what's on the hard drive?"

"One way to find out," Steven said.

They went back to the office to say good-bye to Soames. He waved them quiet and bent closer to his police scanner. "Car accident at Snake Creek," he said. "Some kids went into the water."

Denny immediately thought about Brian, on his way to Miami.

"What kids?" he asked.

"I don't know. A silver Honda. They already took them to the hospital. Why? You know them?"

But they were already out the door.

Chapter Twenty-five

Mariner's Hospital was a long, low building that Denny and Steven both had seen too much of over the years. A patrol car was already in the parking lot. The officer standing in the ER lobby was Sergeant Bonnie Howell, a formidable woman who'd been to barbecues at their house before.

"Is it Brian Vandermark?" Denny asked. "The car accident victim?"

"You know him?" Bonnie fished for the pencil over her ear and noted something in her logbook. "He could use a friend right now."

Denny held his breath as she walked him and Steven back to one of the examination cubicles. Brian was sitting alone on a table, clad in his pants and a paper gown. His right arm hung in a splint and there was a bandage on his forehead.

Denny started toward the table, then stopped. "You okay?"

Brian looked stricken. "Christopher. I think he's hurt badly."

Howell said, "He's in surgery right now."

"I'll go check, if you want," Steven volunteered.

Brian nodded. Steven left, and Denny moved closer to the table. "What happened?"

"Some guy cut us off." Brian sounded more bewildered than angry about it. Denny would have been livid. "Black Toyota, that's all I know."

"They're fishing your car out of the creek and your parents are on their way up," Howell said. "Steven, do you want to keep him company?"

"I'm Denny. Sure I will."

Brian glanced glumly at the splint. "They think it's broken. I'm right-handed."

"I'll sign your cast," Denny promised. *Lame*, he told himself. But Brian didn't seem to notice.

"My car's probably totaled."

"You'll get another." Denny dragged a stool over. "You didn't see the driver?"

Brian shook his head. "Do you think it was on purpose?"

"I don't know. But a lot of strange things seem to be happening around you."

"Why me? When *The Tempest* blew up, I didn't see anything you didn't see."

Denny patted his knee awkwardly, because he didn't want Brian to misinterpret the gesture. And because he really wanted to grab Brian and never let anything bad happen to him again.

It was possible that Denny was totally out of his mind.

Or falling in love.

Luckily, a nurse came in and said, "We're going to go over to X-ray now, see about that arm of yours."

Brian looked uncertainly at Denny.

"I'll be right here when you get back," Denny promised.

"Okay. Thanks."

Left alone, Denny went to find coffee. He was going to need the biggest, hottest cup he could find. All of the vending machines were in the main lobby, which was airy and bright and too cheerful for his taste. A blond man with a crew cut was inserting coins into one slot when Denny got there.

Maybe if he'd been thinking straight, Denny wouldn't have blurted out, "I know you."

The man jerked his head. "What? No."

"You were in Key West. On the boat—"

The man punched Denny in the jaw so hard that Denny spun around and fell backward on the carpeted floor. Pain exploded through his whole face and his vision blurred. Son of a bitch!

The man sprinted away. Denny staggered upright and followed him across the lobby, nearly colliding with a nurse along the way. He could hear concerned voices asking him questions, but they sounded like they were far away and maybe even in a different language.

He burst out past the sliding doors just in time to see Crew Cut ride off on a motorcycle.

A security guard came jogging over. "You all right, kid?"

Denny rubbed his jaw. He was pissed at himself for not seeing that punch coming. Sensei Mike would be embarrassed over him. "Yeah. I'm great."

"Who was that?"

"I'm going to find out." Denny turned to him. "Where are your security tapes?"

In the surgical waiting room, Steven found out that Christopher was under the knife and would be for a while. One of the young nurses at the desk, a brunette with dark blue eyes and perfect skin, flirted with him while he waited.

"So you're in school?" she asked.

"University of Miami," he confirmed.

"You like it?"

"I love it. I'm thinking maybe of becoming a doctor. Specializing in good bedside manners. Any tips?"

She laughed. "I think you're going to have to work on that line."

Her supervisor came over with a dour look. Steven decided to go back to the emergency room. Apparently, chaos had broken out in the time he'd been away—Dad and two of his deputies were standing around Denny, who was holding an ice pack to his jaw. Dad looked pissed off. A hospital security guard was there, too, along with a guy in a tie.

"We'll have prints made up right away," the man in the tie was saying.

"I'm telling you, it was the same guy from Key West," Denny insisted.

Mr. and Mrs. Vandermark arrived before Steven got the full story. Mrs. Vandermark's eyes were puffy and her mascara runny—she'd probably been crying the entire drive up. Mr. Vandermark's expression was stony.

"Your son's fine," Dad told her. "Broken arm, they're already setting it."

Steven sat next to Denny in one of the padded blue chairs.

"He was on the snorkel trip," Denny said. "He never said a word all the way out or back. He could be the same guy who drove Brian off the road."

"You don't know that," Dad said.

"Why else would he punch me and run away?"

"Steven, why don't you take your brother back home? He's going to have to ice that jaw all day."

"I want to stay," Denny said. "I told Brian I'd stay."

"Brian will understand," Dad said firmly. "Don't both of you have to work today?"

Steven checked the clock. "I could switch—"

"Go to work," Dad said. "Brian's parents will take care of him, and people are counting on you."

Steven said, "Okay, but first we have to tell you about what we found at the impound lot."

Halfway through that story, Agent Crown and Agent Garcia arrived. Mr. Vandermark went outside with his cell phone in hand, looking upset. Dad wasn't too pleased to hear they'd opened the SUV but was mollified, at least, that Steven and Denny had left the book and the portable hard drive exactly where they were.

"Give me the keys," Dad said.

Steven handed them over.

"We'll take those," Agent Crown said. "The FBI has jurisdiction here."

"I'm not so sure about that," Dad said.

Which led to a rather heated discussion about who exactly was in charge. Steven thought it was best that they make themselves scarce. He steered Denny out to the parking lot and into the truck.

"I don't want to leave," Denny whined, like a kid.

"You heard Dad. Besides, we're not going to find anything out by sticking around there. Let's call Sensei Mike. Maybe he has friends at the Casa Marina who can fax up a list of everyone who was on that snorkel trip."

Denny said, "Huh. I guess that's a good idea."

"I'm brilliant that way."

Mopey-eyed, Denny watched the hospital recede in the rearview mirror.

"It's just a broken arm, Denny. He'll be fine."

"Someone tried to kill him. That's not fine."

"So we stop them," Steven replied.

Denny met his gaze squarely. "Yeah. We stop them."

CHAPTER TWENTY-SIX

Steven dropped Denny off at the Bookmine. Denny got two feet inside before his mom was all over him.

"They should have taken X-rays! Your father should have insisted," she said. "What if your jaw's broken?"

"My jaw's not broken," he assured her. "I can talk."

Sean Garrity was ringing up purchases for a woman with two small kids. "You got in a fight in the middle of Mariner's Hospital?"

Mom said, "Not now, Sean," and tugged Denny into her office. He always liked it there—small and homey, with vintage travel posters of Cuba on the walls. She sat him down in her chair and peered into his eyes, maybe looking for signs of brain damage.

"I get punched harder in karate class," he said.

"You're lying," Mom said. Today she was dressed in a red dress with yellow fish embroidered all over it. "Do you want some ibuprofen?"

"Sure."

"You should go home and rest."

"I want to work," he said. Besides which, they'd given Mom's fax number for the Casa Marina list, and Denny wanted to be nearby when it came through.

He'd already sent Brian a message, saying he was sorry he had to leave. Brian's first text came an hour after Denny got to the store. He couldn't type well with his left fingers only, but he said he was okay and Christopher was out of surgery with his leg in traction.

Denny apologized again.

Brian sent a picture of his arm in a cast.

Ten minutes later Brian asked, *Did u get punchd?*

Denny said, *I'm fine.*

Brian didn't message anything back.

Mom hovered for hours, but aside from some soreness, Denny felt fine. Part of his job was to work the Buyback desk, where customers could trade in used books for cash or store credit. Several customers brought in overflowing bags, and one brought in a huge cardboard box of hardcover mysteries. Sean kept pestering him as Denny entered the totals into a calculator.

"If you don't tell me what happened, I'll die of curiosity."

Denny replied, "I'll take my chances with your mortality."

"Was it someone's jealous boyfriend?"

"Would you like a black eye?"

Sean wagged his finger. "Violence never solved anything."

"I don't need a solution. I just need silence."

The Casa Marina list didn't come in until three o'clock. There were eighteen names on it, twelve of them male. Crossing off his and Brian's names left him with ten possible suspects. The more he thought about it, the more he was sure that Crew Cut had spoken with an accent—German, maybe. None of the names seemed German, though.

He looked at the last name on the list.

Antonio Ferdinand.

Two more characters in *The Tempest.*

Steven dropped by the sheriff's substation on his way home from lifeguarding. The substation was a brand new building financed by Homeland Security dollars, with gleaming tile floors and state-of-the-art electronics.

Two steps into the lobby and he started to turn around, but it was too late.

"Denny!" said Lucy Mcdaniel.

He faced her. Didn't bother to correct her. "How's the story coming?"

"I wanted to talk to your dad but he's busy," Lucy said. "Something about a car accident? Up the highway?"

"He's got a big jurisdiction."

"I'm trying to finish my story," she said with a little pout. "Can you get me in? Only for ten minutes, I promise."

"I can't."

"I can pay you back. Dinner on me."

"Sorry," Steven said.

Cold anger flashed across her eyes. In that instant, he saw that you never wanted to be the guy who stood her up or broke her heart. Lucy's phone rang and she turned away. He escaped to the front desk, where Sergeant Henry Martin was manning the counter.

"Friend of yours?" Martin was typing into a computer with one hand and squeezing a gel stress toy with the other. "I keep telling her she's not going to get in."

"Dad in a bad mood?"

"Rotten as the bottom shelf of my refrigerator. Go on back."

The captain's office was bigger here than in the old building, with bulletproof windows that looked out on the public baseball field. Steven had played Little League on that field for years and years. Dad was glaring at a whiteboard mounted on the wall.

"What's with the radioactive death stare?" Steven asked.

"I don't like this case," Dad said. "And I don't like that you've been keeping secrets."

Steven kept his poker face on. "Which secrets?"

"You know."

So Dad knew about the Navy. Denny must have said something. Or Eddie Ibarra. He'd have to kill them.

"I was going to tell you," Steven said. "But things just sort of happened fast."

"That money could have given us a clue."

Oh. So this wasn't about the SEALs at all. "Eddie's money?"

"The money Eddie found," Dad said. "What were you thinking, letting them go off and spend all that cash?"

"I didn't know," Steven protested. "I only found out last night, when I was late for curfew. I would have told you, but I didn't want to get him in trouble."

"He came in and reported it himself today," Dad said. "Just after I got back from the hospital. Maybe news of Brian Vandermark's accident scared him into it."

Steven turned around to look at the whiteboard. Written in Dad's neat square handwriting was VANDERMARK, MORGAN, CASA MARINA, TEMPEST, BURGLARY. Dad always did like to work things out in a visual way.

"There's no Agent Prosper working out of the Miami FBI office," Dad said. "So that's an open question."

"Denny thinks maybe it has to do with Shakespeare. There's a guy named Prospero in *The Tempest*."

Dad blinked. "Huh. That's a good one."

"And he texted me a half hour ago. There's a Ferdinand in the play, and a guy named Ferdinand was on that snorkel trip Brian and Denny took in Key West."

Dad picked up a pencil and toyed with it. "I didn't know Brian and Denny were such good friends."

Steven shrugged. "Almost getting killed brings you closer to a guy."

"Is that it?"

He tried not to squirm. "What are you asking me, Dad?"

Dad studied him for a long moment. Out on the baseball field, two kids from the junior high started to toss a ball back and forth.

"Nothing," Dad said with a sigh. "I'll talk to your brother."

Steven was pretty sure he didn't want to be around for that conversation. He turned back to the white board. "What about that SUV that was impounded?"

"We ran the VIN number. It was stolen from Fort Lauderdale last week. The FBI took custody of the hard drive that was in the glove compartment. Obviously, we were meant to find it, sooner or later. Someone wants to communicate something. But it's not my problem anymore."

"The FBI took over?"

"Lock, stock, and barrel," Dad said. "I'd say I'm disappointed, but your mother and I are supposed to go up to that state conference tomorrow and she needs a break from work. You boys should come with us."

"Tallahassee?" Steven shuddered. "That's like going to the desert. You know us, Dad. We'll stay out of trouble."

"You've never been able to stay out of trouble." Dad cocked his head. "You know, you haven't talked about BUD/S much. You're not worried, are you?"

Steven wondered for a moment if Dad knew. Maybe Eddie had spilled more than just the story of the money. Or maybe Dad had run into some of the recruiters from the Miami office. They were always traveling up and down the island, enlisting young people for the navy.

"Sensei Mike says if it doesn't kill me, it'll make me stronger," Steven said cockily. "What do you think?"

"I think you're pretty strong already."

Steven appreciated the thought.

But he still couldn't figure out how to tell his parents that he was lying to them.

CHAPTER TWENTY-SEVEN

Thanks to painkillers, Brian slept the entire afternoon away. He barely remembered Mom driving them home or how he'd crawled right into bed. His dreams were muddy, half-remembered kaleidoscopes of smashing metal and glass. Now, with the sky still blue outside his windows, he dragged himself out of bed and checked his phone. He had twelve text messages from Christopher: *I'm bored, leg hurts, bring me food, where are you,* and several more, not a single one asking Brian how he was.

He adjusted the sling around his arm and went out to find his mother in the kitchen, stirring together whole wheat pasta and organic tomato sauce.

"I made dinner," she said. "How do you feel?"

"Okay. How's Christopher?"

"He's doing fine. Henrik's still up there, trying to arrange for an ambulance to take him back to Boston."

Her words sounded calm, matter-of-fact. Her face was haggard, though, and her shoulders stiff with tension.

He gave her a one-armed hug. "I'm okay, really. It was just a small accident."

"Small!" she exclaimed, into his shoulder. "Small. Tell me that when you've had kids."

"That won't be for a long time," Brian admitted.

She separated from him and drew in a shaky breath. Offered him an equally shaky smile. "Do you need a pill for the pain?"

"I'm good. Starving."

He wasn't really hungry, but finishing the food gave her something to focus on. The two of them ate at the big glass table near the patio doors. He had a hard time eating with only his left hand. Mom pushed her pasta around on her plate and barely touched her garlic bread.

"So we were thinking of going to St. Thomas," she said. "On Thursday."

"Of going where?" he asked, not sure he'd heard correctly.

"St. Thomas."

"In the Caribbean."

"For a little while. Rent a house, lie on the beach, and get away from all this bad karma."

Brian looked at Henrik's empty chair. "Don't we need to stick around and find out who's been behind all this? Breaking into my hotel room, driving us off the road—"

"The FBI is working on it," Mom said. "They don't need us. We'll be somewhere warm and safe, and they can do their jobs. You'll like St. Thomas. It's pretty."

"It's pretty here," Brian argued.

"You don't even like it here."

"I like it fine."

Mom poured herself some wine. "You'll like St. Thomas better. Just for a few weeks. Let things cool down. Please don't argue with me, because it's been a long day."

"I know. I started it off being driven into the ocean."

That was totally the wrong thing to say, because she burst into tears.

So unfair. He could never fight tears.

"I'm sorry," Brian said. "I didn't mean it."

She pressed one hand to her face and waved at him with the other. "You don't know what it's like."

"I'm sorry," he repeated. "Tell me about St. Thomas. What's there to do?"

She sniffed. "There's swimming, and scuba diving, and surfing."

None of which he could do with his arm in a cast.

"Cute boys?" he asked.

She laughed a little. "Yes. Many cute boys."

He tried stabbing more pasta with his fork. "There are some cute boys here. I'd like to stay and hang out, and you guys can go and have a good time."

Mom lifted her head and swallowed her tears. "No. It's not possible."

He stared at her. What aliens had kidnapped his mother and left this clone behind? Last summer she and Henrik had gone to Paris and he'd stayed alone for two weeks in Boston. No parties, no police reports, just a quiet week in which he and Christopher had the whole run of the house for themselves. Mom had called twice a day from France, but at least she hadn't hired a babysitter.

"I don't want to go to St. Thomas," he said slowly, as if that might help her understand. "I'm staying here."

"You can't. We're closing the house up. There won't be any power or water."

"I'll rent a place."

"Don't be silly. That's all I have to say about it. Please don't argue any more. Now's just not the time."

Despite the fact Brian wasn't done with his food, she started clearing the table.

He retreated to his room and texted Denny, who called him back ten minutes later.

"So my mom's gotten totally paranoid," Brian said. "She wants us to go to St. Thomas on Thursday."

"It's not paranoia if someone's really out to get you."

"I'm serious."

"So am I." Denny was silent for a moment. From the background came a strange flapping noise.

Brian asked, "Where are you?"

"On my boat."

"Where's your boat?"

"Heading toward Whale Island."

"Looking for Tom Sawyer's cave?"

"What? No. I needed to get out."

"Come get me," Brian suggested. "I could use some fresh air."

Mom was on her exercise bike in the den, pedaling furiously in front of a TV screen showing a mountain trail. Brian left her a note and went outside in the humid evening to the dock. Denny's sailboat was already drawing near. He brought it in close enough for Brian to step over.

"Hey," Brian said.

"Welcome aboard," Denny replied. He was wearing a dark green shirt and khaki shorts, loose and weatherworn. A bruise marked his chin.

Brian asked, "How's your jaw? I can't believe someone hit you."

"He's lucky I didn't hit him back a lot harder."

"This is your boat, huh?"

"It's actually my dad's. I grew up learning to sail it. Anywhere special you want to go?"

Brian took in a deep breath of the salty air. "Wherever you want to go."

Denny steered them toward Whale Island. He was due for a haircut and the tips of curls blew back slightly from his forehead. His eyes were unreadable behind sunglasses and Brian wanted to reach over, slide them away.

"How's Douchebag?" Denny asked.

"He's bored and wants visitors. Want to go visit with me tomorrow?"

"Do you want me to?"

Brian thought about it and shook his head. "You'd probably drive up Christopher's blood pressure just by being there."

Denny steered them away from land and northward along the coast. Brian liked watching his easy confidence, his suntanned face. He caught himself staring and forced his gaze away, determined not to make Denny uneasy.

"Some stuff happened today with your case," Denny said, and told him about finding the keys, discovering the portable hard drive, and figuring out the names from Shakespeare's play.

"The last owners of *The Tempest* were from Denmark," Denny added. "I don't know how that adds in."

"We'd need to ask Prince Hamlet. *The Tempest* was set near Italy," Brian said. "I don't know any Italians."

"Me, neither."

The sun was on the other side of the sky, below Fisher Key's treetops as it sank into the Gulf. The clouds over their heads reflected pink and gold. Brian would miss the tropical sunsets when he was gone. Boston had a lot of great things going for it, but not sunsets.

And no Denny Anderson either. Who was currently nudging Brian's foot.

"Huh?" Brian asked.

"You zoned out on me."

"I'm enjoying the peace and quiet and the company."

Denny adjusted the sail and looked away.

Brian watched the waves moving by underneath them and the birds flapping over their heads toward land. He didn't want there to be awkwardness between them. He started to babble to fill the silence.

"I told you I knew by fifth grade that I was gay," Brian said. "But I didn't tell anyone until a lot later. I couldn't. Once you say it you can't take it back. It's like a nuclear explosion. There's a flash and heat and then fallout for years. I was sure I'd tell the wrong person and they'd blab it all over school. Maybe everyone could tell anyway, but I walked around keeping it inside. Me and my secret in the halls of Jefferson Junior High."

"Eventually you told someone," Denny said, sounding distant.

"I went to a private high school. Governor Winthrop Academy. Big campus. Old ivy. The third day of school, I'm lost between buildings and can't find my next class. I'm sure that everyone can see what a dork I am and that I'm going to fail out miserably. This other freshman comes up to me with his tie undone and jacket all crooked. He says, 'I hereby appoint you a charter member of the Gay Club I'm starting.' That was Christopher."

Adjusting the tiller, Denny said, "So you didn't have to tell him. He figured it out."

"He claims to have excellent gaydar."

"Do you have excellent gaydar?"

"Nope. Sometimes I need to be hit by the clue bus. You?"

Denny shrugged.

"I had to tell my grandparents. They didn't believe me."

Denny snorted. "They thought you were wrong?"

"They thought I was confused. Grandma eventually came around. Grandpa still doesn't believe it. But being gay wasn't something I could hide forever anyway, so I'm glad it's out there."

Denny was quiet. Brian figured he'd pushed hard enough. You shouldn't make someone else come out. They had to find their own way to do it, on their own schedule. But that didn't stop him from wanting to kiss Denny right there, to lick the salt from his lips and throat.

The weather was perfect for sailing, with a good breeze and calm sea. Brian didn't know how to sail, which Denny told him was pretty tragic. He taught Brian how to tack and follow the navigation buoys near the marina. Brian began to get cold, but he didn't want any of it to end—the wind and water, Denny so handsome, the two of them on a sturdy boat far from land.

"Uh oh," Denny said.

Brian followed his gaze to a spinning red light on land. A police car was parked outside of his house, and rectangular white light spilled out of the open front door.

"Mom!" Brian exclaimed.

As soon as they reached the dock he leapt over and sprinted toward the house. Denny called out, "Wait for me!" but Brian couldn't. When he reached the house he found Mom standing in the kitchen with Officer Lyle Horne taking notes beside her. Mom was crying again.

"But he wouldn't just leave—" she was saying.

"Mom! What's going on?"

"Oh, Brian!" She flung herself on him despite his broken arm. "You're okay!"

"Of course I'm okay," he said, grimacing as the sling shifted and pain raced up into his shoulder. "I went out. I left you a note."

She wiped her face. "I wasn't sure it was real."

Denny had arrived and was standing behind Brian. He said, "Maybe you don't need the police anymore, Mrs. Vandermark."

Lyle shot Denny a dark look.

"Thank you, Officer," she said to Lyle. "I appreciate your hard work."

"Yes, ma'am," he said.

Lyle let himself out. Brian said, "I can't believe you called the police. I'm eighteen. I went out."

"You don't know everything I'm dealing with," Mom said.

"Mrs. Vandermark, is there anything we can help you with? My dad's really good at his job. He can be here in ten minutes if there's something you want to tell him."

Brian wondered what Denny meant. Mom just dabbed at her eyes and wouldn't look at him directly.

"I'm fine, Denny. We're all fine. Thank you, though. I appreciate it."

Brian pulled her close to his uninjured side. "Thanks for the boat ride. I'll talk to you tomorrow, okay?"

"Sure," Denny said. "Good night, Mrs. Vandermark."

Brian wanted to walk him to the door. Thank him again. Look at him one more time before he went out into the night.

Instead he stood and comforted his mother as she cried against his shoulder.

CHAPTER TWENTY-EIGHT

When Denny reached home, Steven and Kelsey were swimming in the lagoon under the stars. Kelsey was wearing her bathing suit and Steven had on his jean shorts. They laughed and splashed at each other as Denny tied up the boat.

"Come on in, Denny, the water's fine," Kelsey said.

"Moonlight skinny dipping?" Denny asked.

"Not enough moon," Steven replied, kissing Kelsey's neck, "But I could totally get into the skinny dipping part."

She laughed. "I bet you could."

Denny tried not to wish he and Brian were the ones slipping and sliding over each other in the water. Self-discipline really sucked.

"I just came from the Vandermarks," he said. "They're leaving town on Thursday. Going to St. Thomas."

Kelsey hooked one arm around Steven's neck. "Oh! I love the Virgin Islands."

Did she have to say virgin?

"I think I need some ice cream," Denny said and headed for the house.

Mom was packing for the trip to Tallahassee. "What do you think, this dress or this one?" she asked Denny. She held up two equally flamboyant dresses that made her look like tropical birds.

"You never ask Steven for fashion advice," he said.

"Have you seen what he wears?"

Steven and Kelsey came up from the lagoon, lured by the idea of ice cream. There actually wasn't much in the freezer so Steven said, "Let's go to the Dreamette. Come on, Denny."

He didn't want to be a third wheel, but the idea of soft-serve chocolate with caramel was too tempting. Besides, it was better to go out than mope at home over his total inability to ever kiss Brian Vandermark.

Besides, he liked Kelsey. She was smart and funny, even if she had beaten him for valedictorian by the tiniest fraction of a grade.

It wasn't her fault that his love life was non-existent, but did she have to keep touching Steven?

The Dreamette was a concrete building at the end of the island, near the bridge that spanned over to Pirate's Key. Music spilled out of the parking lot speakers, and picnic tables filled the grassy lot near the cars. They ran into lots of kids from school there, including Sean and Robin. Robin hadn't seen the bruise darkening on Denny's jaw.

"You want me to beat up whoever did it?" she asked.

"Stand in line," Steven said.

Jennifer O'Malley was there, too, in her red Corvette. When Denny came out of the bathroom she was waiting for him.

She threw her arms around his neck and planted a big sloppy kiss on his mouth.

"I had a great time yesterday," she murmured.

He tried not to show how grossed out he was. "I'm not Steven."

"Oh!" Jennifer stepped back. "I couldn't tell."

"Now you can."

She walked away without answering.

Later, after they dropped Kelsey off at her house, Denny turned and punched Steven in the arm.

"Hey!" Steven yelped. "What was that for?"

"What did you do with Jennifer yesterday?"

Steven turned his attention back to the dark road. Lamp posts were infrequent on this side of the island. "I don't know what you mean."

"She told me."

"She wouldn't."

"She thought I was you."

"And now I'm insulted."

"You slept with her while you're still seeing Kelsey!"

"It was an accident!"

"How do you accidentally sleep with someone?"

Steven braked as they reached the Overseas Highway. "Because it just happened."

"Oh, it just happened," Denny mocked. "Officer, I didn't mean to rob that bank. It just happened."

"She tortured me all day with her tiny bikini and big breasts," Steven said. "You don't know what that's like."

"No, how would I know, I'm just the idiot who can't even kiss a guy. So not fair!"

"I thought this was about Jennifer and me."

"It is!" Denny exclaimed and then looked past Steven into the parking lot of the Li'l Conch Cafe. "Oh."

"What is it?" Steven asked.

Denny nodded. Nathan Carter and Agent Garcia were standing at the corner of the building, next to a white Ford that was probably Garcia's.

"They must be getting back together," Denny said.

"You don't know that."

Carter and Garcia were both dressed casually, in long pants and short-sleeved shirts. Carter was a little taller than Garcia, Garcia a little wider in the shoulders. They made a good-looking couple, Denny thought morosely.

"Drive," he told Steven.

"Don't you want to see them kiss?"

"I want to hold you underwater until you drown. Drive."

Steven turned onto the highway.

Despite himself, Denny turned to watch through the back window. They were standing awfully close to each other, but they didn't kiss.

He forced himself to stop watching. "Did you ask Carter about the waiver?"

"No."

"Why not?"

"I'm not interested."

"That's the biggest, fattest lie you've ever told," Denny said.

"Really?" Steven perked up. "You think?"

"You don't get an award."

"I should get something," Steven said.

"Karma's on its way," Denny promised.

CHAPTER TWENTY-NINE

Nathan Carter was sitting on the deck of the *Idle* with pieces of a bilge pump spread on the newspaper in front of him. "You're up early," Carter said. "Get an eyeful last night?"

Steven had rolled out of bed at dawn, run five miles up and down the Overseas Highway, and was now dripping sweat and guzzling water on the dock beside Carter's boat. He'd told himself he wasn't going to come by, but here he was.

"I don't care about your love life," Steven said. "Kind of a coincidence, though. Him being the FBI agent assigned to the case."

"Not a coincidence. I called in a favor. The FBI was coming anyway, but I wanted someone who was good at his job."

Steven walked back and forth, keeping his muscles warm. The planks creaked under his feet. "You told my brother there was a way to get a waiver. For someone who failed the color test."

"I served with someone who did."

"But what if he had to tell some colors apart on a map or a machine?"

Carter wiped grease off his hands. "His vision was fine. Drop him in the middle of the Amazon, he could tell you a hundred different shades of green. The military test didn't work for him."

Steven tried not to feel hope.

"If you want it, don't let one test and one doctor stop you," Carter said. "Raise hell until your dying breath."

Steven drank more water.

Carter picked up a wrench. "Or maybe your heart's not really in it."

"Bullshit. I've been getting ready for years."

"Yeah? How many push-ups can you do right now?"

"A hundred good ones."

"Prove it."

Steven dropped down and powered through his push-ups. The only sounds were the seagulls, his own breathing, and the occasional clink of metal as Carter kept working on the pump. The muscles in his arms and shoulders began to ache, then burn, then scream out a protest, but he wasn't kidding. He'd been practicing long before Nathan Carter ever showed up on Fisher Key.

He didn't expect Carter to applaud him when he was done, but did he have to look so bored?

"What about sit-ups?" Carter asked.

Steven did a hundred sit-ups. Sweat blinded his eyes and his abs protested the abuse but he powered through.

"How fast can you run?" Carter asked when Steven had finished.

"I can do the Seven Mile Bridge run in forty minutes."

Carter allowed, "It's a start."

"A start! It's better than that."

"Your form's sloppy," Carter said, unfazed by Steven's indignation. "A good drill instructor would throw out at least twenty of those push-ups. You can run, but how fast is your mile when you've got boots on and fifty pounds in your backpack? I haven't even seen your pull-ups or swimming."

"You're full of it," Steven said, which maybe wasn't the most respectful thing to say to a guy who could kill him with his little finger.

"Maybe. Only one way to find out for sure."

"How's that?"

"Get into BUD/S and pass the tests."

Steven pulled himself to his feet. "First I need that waiver."

Carter examined a piece of the pump. "Come back in a month, and if you can pass the PT test—my version of it—I'll recommend your waiver to some people I know. They can help."

"I don't need a month. I'll be back in two weeks."

Carter snickered. "Hotshot."

Although it hadn't rung, Carter picked up his cell phone. "Yeah, Carter here."

A woman's fast, high voice blasted out of the phone loud enough for Steven to hear it on the dock—no exact words, but someone sure sounded upset.

Carter said, "Okay, calm down. I'll be right over."

He hung up. "Gotta go, kid. Why don't you run on home and practice those push-ups?"

Steven promised, "I'll see you in two weeks."

Denny made French toast for breakfast. Mom was rushing around, stuffing last-minute items into her suitcase. Dad sat at the kitchen table looking calm and firm.

"I mean it," he repeated to Denny.

"But the FBI's just going to mess it up," he complained. "You never trust them."

"It's their jurisdiction," Dad repeated. "Their case. Stay out of it. They'll protect Brian and his family."

"They weren't protecting him last night," Denny protested. "There wasn't anyone watching the house."

"Just because you didn't see anyone doesn't mean they weren't there."

The French toast was beginning to burn. Denny said, "Mrs. Vandermark called nine-one-one. She wouldn't have done that if she had the FBI camping outside."

Dad shook his head. "You don't know everything that's going on, and it's not your business anymore. Let Agent Crown and Agent Garcia do their jobs."

Mom poked her head out of the bathroom. "Who stole my hair dryer?"

"Not me," Denny said. "Dad—"

"Dennis Andrew, do you want me to cancel this trip with your mother just to stay here and babysit you?"

Threats like that were so unfair. Denny didn't know how to make his father understand that this case was personal. He couldn't stand by and just let something awful happen to Brian.

Dad's voice hardened. "Do you?"

"No, sir."

"And I don't want to hear any complaints about you from the FBI when I get back, either," Dad said.

Steven returned from his morning run looking drenched and exhausted. He headed immediately for the refrigerator. "Who's complaining?"

"No one," Dad said. "Make sure it stays that way. Steven, you're older. You're in charge."

Denny protested, "That's not fair! I'm the more responsible one."

"No, you're just the more emo one." Steven grabbed a bottle of apple juice and swallowed down large gulps. "You can count on me, Dad."

Denny flattened the French toast with his spatula and let it burn.

Brian woke with his arm aching. He stared at the ceiling, disoriented. Was he in the hospital? Back in Boston? No, this was his bedroom in Florida. He had a smashed car and a broken arm and his mom wanted to drag him to St. Thomas.

He pulled his pillow over his head.

It took a while to get out of bed, use the bathroom, and put on unwrinkled clothes. The damn cast made everything twice as hard. He thought he heard Mom and Henrik talking in the living room, but when he went out there, he saw Nathan Carter sitting on the sofa and drinking fresh-squeezed orange juice. The curtains had been drawn against the sun, and the air-conditioning seemed even colder than usual.

"Brian, you remember Mr. Carter," Mom said from the kitchen counter.

"Call me Nathan," Carter said, rising to shake Brian's hand.

"Where's Henrik?" Brian asked.

Mom said, "He's in St. Thomas already. Waiting for us. Nathan's going to drive us up to say good-bye to Christopher, then help us pack and get to the airport."

"You said we weren't leaving until Thursday," Brian said, confused.

"Plans have changed," Carter said. "We're leaving in a half-hour for the hospital, if you want to grab some breakfast first."

Brian looked from Carter to his mom and then back again. "She hired you to be our chauffeur?"

"Not so much with the chauffeuring," Carter said. "I'm just around to make sure things go well."

"Mom?"

"Mr. Carter used to be in the Navy, you know," Mom said from the kitchen. "He's very organized."

Brian needed coffee if he was going to deal with any of this. He got himself some coffee and then retreated to his bedroom. He was more than surprised when Carter followed him in.

"It's best to keep your curtains closed," Carter said. "Your room is directly exposed to the ocean. It's a liability."

Brian stared at him. "You're not serious."

"Do I look like I'm joking?"

"Someone's going to climb up the side of the building and break in?"

"A sniper could shoot you through the glass."

"That's crazy!" Brian exclaimed. "Don't you think my mother is overreacting?"

Carter didn't blink. "I think you should let me do my job."

"What is your job?"

"Protect you and your mother from now until you get on that plane."

Carter's expression was set in stone. Brian had never met someone more deadly serious in his entire life.

"Fine. I'll let you do your job. Can I go to the bathroom now? Alone?"

"Sure."

Brian retreated to the bathroom, closed the door, and texted Denny.

CHAPTER THIRTY

Denny opened the Bookmine at ten a.m. for a handful of customers already clustered in the parking lot. He welcomed them into the store as if he personally owned it. It wasn't the first time he'd been in charge while his mother was away, but usually Dad was on the island, too. Now both of them were off to Tallahassee, though not without a few annoying reminders: be safe, no parties, listen to Steven.

That last part really irked. Steven? Who was busy lying to them about his enlistment and cheating on Kelsey with Jennifer?

No, he wouldn't be listening to Steven.

Sean and Robin showed up ten minutes later, bearing doughnuts and iced coffees. Sugar and caffeine made Denny forgive them for their tardiness.

Brian sent him a frantic message at quarter past ten: *call me urgent mom's gone crazy.*

Denny let Sean handle the next customer and retreated to the privacy of Mom's office. Over the phone he asked, "What's wrong?"

Brian sounded unhappy. "We're leaving for St. Thomas tonight."

"What? Why?"

"I don't know. And get this: she hired Nathan Carter as some kind of bodyguard."

"She did?"

"He's here right now."

Denny listened to the background noise. "What's that sound?"

"The shower."

Denny sat up straighter. "You're calling me from the shower?"

"The only place I can get some privacy is in the bathroom."

Unbidden images of Brian naked under streaming hot water made it hard for Denny to concentrate.

"We're leaving to go see Christopher in a few minutes." Brian's voice dropped. "I'd rather see you."

Denny didn't know what to say to that. Shower water ran in the background like a waterfall as words and possibilities stretched between them.

"You still there?"

"Yeah. I'm at the Bookmine. Tell your Mom that one of your special order books came in and you want to pick it up before you go."

"Think they'll buy it?"

"You can try."

"I will. I promise."

Denny hung up. Why did Mrs. Vandermark want to leave tonight? They couldn't just fly off like that. Not when Denny was just beginning to think he'd have all summer to hang out with Brian. Maybe Brian could stay behind? He was eighteen years old, not some kid. But where? Sleep on Denny's sofa? Get his own apartment?

They had to be leaving because of *The Tempest*. Everything had started with that one boat.

Or started with the play, Denny thought.

Out in the store, Sean was busy with a couple of tourists and Robin was signing for some boxes from the delivery man. Cars whizzed by on the Overseas Highway in a blur of noise and color. Not too many customers in the shop.

"I'll be in the Shakespeare section," he said.

They had four copies of *The Tempest* in stock, including a leather-bound hardcover and a yellowed paperback from the 1950s. Denny took the paperback and sat on the floor.

The play started with a shipwreck caused by a tempest. The Florida Keys had a colorful history of wrecks and storms, but none lately.

Two brothers. One usurped by the other. The usurped one in exile with his daughter on an island.

On second thought, maybe this was all a dead end.

No. Someone had blown up that yacht. If not for insurance, then for revenge. But if Denny was going to blow up a boat, he'd do it in Key West or Miami, some place with a strong local media. The last owners had been Danish and the boat had been stolen in France.

He pulled out his cell phone and called Channel 4 in Miami.

It took fifteen minutes of getting transferred around before he reached Janet Hogan.

"This better be good, kid," she said.

"If I'm right, it'll be a big story," Denny said. "Remember we told you *The Tempest* was stolen?"

"That was a week ago. That's light years in a news cycle."

"A light year is distance, not time," he said.

"Did you call me to play Mr. Science Geek?"

Denny grimaced. "Who owned it when it was stolen?"

"Some couple from Copenhagen, so what?"

"Who did they get it from?"

"Like I remember," Janet said huffily. He heard the clicking of a keyboard. "They bought it from a family-owned business in Denmark. Big into diamonds until one of the owners got arrested for smuggling and went to jail."

What had Brian said about his stepfather?

He'd made his fortune in jewelry.

"What's the name of the man who went to jail?"

"You're going to owe me for this, you know that?"

"I pay my debts," Denny said. "What's his name?"

Nathan Carter drove Brian and his mother up to Mariner's Hospital in Mom's Mercedes. Brian chafed like a little kid riding in the backseat. He was surprised to see Agent Garcia sitting in the waiting room outside Christopher's room.

"Nothing all night," Garcia reported.

Christopher started complaining the minute he saw Brian.

"—and forget trying to get any sleep. All the nurses do around here is talk all night, and they wake you up every four hours for no reason at all, and did you bring me coffee? Real coffee? The coffee here sucks—"

Brian eyed the complicated-looking device holding Christopher's leg elevated. A modern-day torture device. He suddenly felt sorry for him. "Does it hurt?"

"What do you think?"

Nathan Carter said, "The ambulance should be here within an hour. They'll take you up to Miami for the air ambulance."

"What if I get airsick?" Christopher complained.

"You won't," Mom promised. "I brought you some ginger to suck on."

Christopher complained up until the point the paramedics closed the doors. When he was gone, Brian expected to feel relieved. Instead, getting back into Mom's car, he only felt depressed. He wanted to go back to bed and sleep for days.

But he'd promised Denny.

"Can we swing by the Bookmine on the way home?" he asked his mother.

"We really have to pack, honey."

"It won't be long. I have to pick up a book I ordered. They won't have it in St. Thomas."

Mom looked at Carter, who pulled the car smoothly into traffic. "We need to tell you something first. I should have told you yesterday, but everything's happening so fast—I'm sorry."

For a wild, irrational moment Brian thought she was going to tell him she was having an affair with Carter. Which was stupid crazy, even if Carter was straight. Mom loved Henrik the way she loved health food and yoga and maybe even Brian.

"It's about Henrik," Mom said. "Why he had to leave. Why we have to leave, too. I know you think I've been overreacting, but when your family is threatened, well, I hope you never have to make choices like this."

"Mom, you're scaring me," Brian said.

She reached over the seat to hold his good hand. "I'm scared, too. But everything is going to be okay. I promise."

CHAPTER THIRTY-ONE

With his parents off to Tallahassee and Denny at work, Steven was enjoying a rare morning alone. Too bad his phone was filling up with messages from Kelsey and Jennifer both. He called Eddie.

"Let's go kayaking."

"Huh?" Eddie sounded only half-awake. "Where?"

"Doesn't matter."

It took an hour for Eddie to show up. His red T-shirt smelled rank and he needed to shave, but he seemed clear-headed enough. They carried the kayaks from the shed down into the crystal-blue water and set off across the lagoon. The outbound tide carried them south toward the old military fort at Mercy Key, but they only got as far as Flagler's old bridge before Eddie wanted to stop for lunch.

They pulled the kayaks up onto the thin shore of Pirate's Key and ate the turkey sandwiches Steven had made. Flagler's bridge stretched south beside the modern construction that carried the Overseas Highway. It was off-limits these days except for fisherman. Looking up, Steven could see a few old men dangling lines into the water.

"My dad told me you confessed about the money," Steven said.

Eddie yawned. "I guess I had to. Lisa was pissed, though. We fought all night long. She threw me out of my own bed."

"Your mom lets her stay over?"

"She doesn't know. She's working nights at Sal's and cleaning houses all day."

Steven popped open a cherry soda and squinted out at the water. He wanted to suggest that Eddie get a job, too, but he didn't know how to lifeguard, he'd been fired from Sal's Gas & Go last summer, and the Dreamette only hired sixteen-year-old girls who wore low-cut tops. He was good with computers, but not much better than anyone else their age.

"My mother cleans house for your fag friend," Eddie said.

"Shut up with that talk unless you want to swim back," Steven said.

"Why so touchy?"

"Because it's not right."

"What, you don't think they don't hear it in the real world?"

Steven drank more soda. It tasted more sour than sweet. "Real world, this world, doesn't matter."

"They're a crazy family anyway," Eddie said. "Always fighting."

"The Vandermarks? About what?"

"Something about money and his family back in Europe. Big scandal, someone was in prison."

"Who?"

"I don't know. I think they're all in witness protection or something."

Sometimes you couldn't tell whether Eddie was making stuff up or just getting things wrong.

"They change your name in witness protection," Steven said. "And you don't get visits from old friends in Boston."

"Gay boyfriends, you mean."

"Get off the gay thing."

Eddie rummaged around in the cooler they had brought. "Mom heard them arguing about that boat, too. The one that blew up. Why didn't you bring beer?"

"What about the boat?" Steven asked.

"Something about how it all started with that boat, and look what Poul did—no, I don't know who Poul is—and how he wasn't going to stop, that it was just the beginning. Didn't you know? Mr. Vandermark used to own it."

❖

As lunchtime came and went, Denny was worried that he'd never see Brian again. Then, just after one o'clock, they all showed up—Brian, his mother, and Nathan Carter.

Under other circumstances, Denny would have been overjoyed to see Carter in the store. But today he only had eyes for Brian, who looked pale and nervous.

"I'm here for my order," Brian said.

"It's somewhere back in my Mom's office," Denny replied. "I'll show you."

Brian said to Carter, "I'll be in there. Don't hover."

Carter eyed Denny. He didn't say anything, but he obviously wasn't going anywhere.

"Sure, honey," said Mrs. Vandermark. "We'll wait."

Denny led Brian into the office and closed the door. "I figured it out. Your stepdad's family used to own *The Tempest*. It was blown up on purpose to send a message to him."

Brian grimaced. "I know."

"You know?" Denny's excitement deflated like a punctured balloon. "Since when?"

"Since about a half hour ago," Brian said. "Mom told me everything on the way back from the hospital. Henrik's got a brother, Poul, who's been threatening us over some old family dispute about the business."

"Poul Damgaard was arrested and convicted of smuggling diamonds and tax evasion while running the family jewelry business," Denny explained. "While he was in jail, his younger brother sold the business and its assets. No one knows what happened to him. He must have come to America and changed his name—and married your mother."

"I don't know everything," Brian said. "I don't even think my mother knows. After the accident yesterday, Henrik agreed to meet Poul in Miami to withdraw money. But most of the money is in the Virgin Islands, so now we're supposed to meet them there."

"What does the FBI say?"

"They're not involved."

"What?" Denny realized his voice was too loud. He lowered it. "My dad said the FBI took over."

"Mom says Henrik told her not to cooperate with them. That's why she hired Carter. Carter's friend Agent Garcia guarded Christopher last night in the hospital only as a favor. Otherwise, I'm not supposed to talk to any police or federal agents."

Someone knocked on the door.

"You okay in there?" Carter asked.

"Yeah!" Brian said. "Be right out."

Denny wanted to step forward and touch him, but he didn't. "You don't have to go with them. You can stay here on Fisher Key."

"I have to take care of my mom," Brian said ruefully.

"It's dangerous! How do you know things will go okay in St. Thomas?"

Brian said, "I don't know. But I have to go."

Outside in the store, someone laughed at the counter. Denny wanted to reach through the wall and throttle them.

"Thanks for everything," Brian said. "Even though you're not you-know-what. It's been nice to have one friend on this island."

"You have more than one," Denny protested.

"Not really. But I wish—well, whatever."

Brian lifted his chin, stared straight at Denny. Denny worried he was going to lean forward and kiss him. Maybe "worried" wasn't the right word. Hoped? Because there they were, standing in the small office just an arm's length apart, Brian with his blue eyes and dorky glasses, his expression determined. Denny suddenly wanted to taste him—his lips, the skin along his jaw, the hollow of his throat. He wanted to grab him and keep him, like a prize or a treasure no one else could have.

"Don't freak out, okay?" Brian said.

Then he stepped forward and kissed Denny on the cheek. Brief, soft, but like an electric jolt that went right down the length of Denny's body.

Brian took a step backward. "I gotta go."

And then he walked right out of Denny's life.

CHAPTER THIRTY-TWO

Steven and Eddie kayaked home, Steven leading the way over the choppy waves. He hadn't been paying much attention to the marine forecast, but clouds had started to appear in the southwest and the wind had picked up. *Storm on the way*, he thought. For now the sun was shining and hot against his face. As he pulled into the lagoon he saw Kelsey sitting on the end of the dock. She'd pulled the garden hose down from the house and was rinsing off her feet.

"Hey!" he called out.

She smiled, waved, and waited until he got within a few feet. Then she squirted the water hose at his face full blast.

"You snake!" she yelled.

He threw up his arms to fend off the water and succeeded in capsizing into the water. For a moment, floating in the murky blue-green, he considered staying underwater for, oh, forever. More or less.

Kelsey Carlson: Most Likely to Be Really Pissed Off.

He surfaced, only to have a car sponge tossed at him next. A bucket sat on the dock beside her. Who knew what else she had in there?

"You total lying jerk!" she shouted. "You slept with Jennifer!"

Eddie stopped his kayak a safe distance away. "Jennifer? Really?"

A garden pot plopped into the water beside Steven's head. Tin, not terra cotta.

"You slept with her and you didn't think I'd find out?" Kelsey shrieked, her face red.

Steven had no good answer. "I'm sorry!"

"You're more than sorry." Kelsey reached into the bucket and pulled out a bottle of plant fertilizer. All stuff from Mom's garden. "You're a creep!"

"Don't pollute the water—" Steven started, then had to duck the fertilizer. He scooped it up before it began to leak, found his footing in the lagoon sand, and reached for the hull of the kayak. "Come on. Stop throwing stuff."

Kelsey picked up a hand shovel and eyed him vengefully.

"Aren't you even going to say you're sorry?"

"I did!"

"Say it again."

"I'm sorry. I was wrong. It was stupid. You have every right to be furious with me."

"I'm more than furious," Kelsey said.

Eddie's phone rang.

"Hello? Huh? Okay. Ten minutes." He hung up. "Lisa's car is broken down at the Gas & Go. Can I get out of the water or are you going to throw something at me, too?"

Kelsey said, "It depends. Did you know about this?"

"No," Steven said.

"No, but I'm not surprised," Eddie said.

Steven swung around in the water to him. "Why not?"

"You know," Eddie said, looking uncomfortable. "You like girls."

Kelsey threw a conch shell at him.

Eddie dragged his kayak up on the sand to escape her and took off on his bike, saying, "Call me later!" Eventually Kelsey ran out of things to throw at Steven and got back into her car and left him in the lagoon, surrounded by debris like the survivor of a shipwreck.

A wreck he'd caused on his own.

He didn't think Kelsey was likely to forgive him anytime soon.

He couldn't blame her.

CHAPTER THIRTY-THREE

B rian climbed into the back of his mother's car wanting to scream and shout at the unfairness of it all.

Mom turned around from her seat. "Okay, honey?"

Carter's gaze met Brian's in the rearview mirror.

"Sure," he said woodenly.

They returned to the house, where Mrs. Ibarra had been busy filling boxes and suitcases for them. Mom took over like an army general. Brian started to pack shorts and shirts, but he'd rather have his books. He could always buy clothes in St. Thomas, right?

The phone rang twice with calls that Mom took in the study. Carter prowled the house looking for trouble. At some point he'd put on a holster, and the sight of the gun made Brian's stomach twist.

It wasn't a dream, or some paranoid fantasy. Someone really wanted to hurt his mother, hurt him. Not just some stranger, but Henrik's own brother. What had happened between them to cause such animosity years later?

Mrs. Ibarra made a late lunch for everyone and promised Mom she'd take care of the food in the refrigerator so it wouldn't go to waste. Then she pulled off her apron, saying, "I have to be at the gas station by three. I'll come back tomorrow, take care of everything."

"Thank you," Mom said and kept packing.

At four thirty a UPS truck picked up the sealed boxes. The large furniture and all the rest of their stuff would have to wait until they sent for it. Brian looked out at the sunlight on the Atlantic and tried not to regret leaving a place he'd always intended to leave anyway.

"Time to go," Mom said at five o'clock.

"But the plane doesn't leave from Miami until nine," Brian protested.

"We're not going to Miami," Carter said. "That was just for other people to think. Your stepfather chartered a private jet out of Marathon. It leaves in an hour."

Brian turned to his mother. "Are we even going to St. Thomas?"

She shook her head. "Cayman Islands."

"Why doesn't anyone tell me the truth?" Brian demanded.

"Because it's not about you, kid," Carter said. "Let's go."

The doorbell rang.

"You expecting anyone?" Carter asked quietly.

Mom shook her head. Brian echoed the gesture.

Carter reached for his gun, motioned for them to stay back, and edged toward the door. After checking the peephole, he relaxed and opened the door for Eddie Ibarra.

Brian hadn't seen Eddie since he'd been drunk on graduation night. He looked worse now—pale, shaky, in need of a shave.

"Is my mom still here?" he asked. "She didn't show up for work at the gas station."

Mom covered her mouth with her hand. "Oh, no."

Carter asked, "You've called her?"

"There's no answer," Eddie said. "She always answers."

Carter reached for his pocket. "I'll call my friend—"

He turned away from the door.

Eddie Ibarra shot him.

❖

For a moment, nothing made sense to Brian. The pistol in Eddie's hand looked real, but the sound was more of a sizzle than a pop. Carter stumbled, fell, convulsed on the floor. No blood, though.

Stun gun, he realized.

Eddie had shot Carter with a Taser.

Brian's head told him to run, but his feet wouldn't move. Mom actually stepped forward, one hand reaching out.

"What are you doing?"

"Mom!" Brian grabbed her before Eddie could shoot her, too.

"I'm sorry," Eddie said. "I had to! I'm sorry!"

Despite the shock, Carter reached for the counter and started to haul himself upward.

Movement in the doorway made Brian's head snap around. He didn't recognize the young woman in the doorway but her gun was real. Despite the silencer on the end, it made a loud noise when it fired.

The impact of the bullet threw Carter backward, blood blossoming across his chest.

Brian stepped in front of his mother to protect her.

"Hello, Brian," the stranger said. "It's nice to meet you. I'm your cousin, Miranda."

CHAPTER THIRTY-FOUR

Denny came home from the Bookmine at five o'clock and slumped down on the sofa.

"There's a bucket floating in the lagoon," he said.

Steven didn't take his eyes off the TV. The news had come on, and Janet Hogan was blathering about something or other. He couldn't remember what he'd watched before the news, but it hadn't been very interesting.

"Kelsey threw it at me. She found out about Jennifer."

"Oh."

"That's it? Oh? No gloating?"

"Brian's stepdad is being blackmailed and they're all on their way to St. Thomas."

That made Steven look up. "Blackmail?"

"Family feud, extortion, and they don't want the FBI involved at all. They're gone."

Steven thought about that. "Did you kiss good-bye?"

"Shut up."

"You did, didn't you?" Steven sat up. "You did it!"

Denny blushed. "No. He did it. One kiss, on the cheek. In Mom's office."

"You know, Mom put a closed-circuit camera in the ceiling there last month—"

Denny threw a sofa pillow at him.

Neither felt like cooking, so they went to the Li'l Conch Cafe for hamburgers and fries. The food sat on their plates, mostly untouched, while Denny explained what Brian had told him.

"I can't believe he's just gone now," Denny said. "I might never see him again."

"At least you didn't sleep with him and cheat on him and break his heart," Steven said.

"You didn't break Kelsey's heart."

"How do you know?"

"She's smart. She had to know that you're you."

"What does that mean? What am I? A serial cheater?"

Denny gave him a level look. "Since when have you ever dated anyone for longer than two months?"

Sean Garrity's sister Louanne came over to check on their drinks. She frowned at them both.

"Something wrong with the food tonight?"

"No, the food's fine," Steven said glumly.

Denny added, "We'll take it to go."

She boxed it up, they paid the bill, and stepped outside to a sky that had grown gray and cloudy. No brilliant sunset would light up the west tonight. Steven smelled rain in the distance.

"How does it end?" Steven asked.

"What?"

"The play."

Denny said, "You read it in ninth grade."

"No, you read it in ninth grade. I copied your homework when you weren't looking."

They crossed the gravel parking lot. Denny said, "It's a comedy, so everything ends happily. The brothers are reconciled, the girl gets her man, and everyone goes back to Italy."

"What girl?"

"Miranda. She's the daughter of the exiled brother, Prospero."

Steven slid behind the driver's wheel. "So Poul thinks he's Prospero. Where's his daughter?"

"I don't know. If she's around, she hasn't shown herself. Unless…"

Steven turned the ignition. "Unless what, Shakespeare?"
Denny said, "Unless she has, and we didn't notice."

❖

"I'm sorry," Eddie kept saying. "They said they'd kill Lisa and my mom. They took them somewhere—"

Miranda said, "Yes, yes, your angst is very interesting. Aunt Hannah, will you do the honors and tie his hands behind his back using these?"

She tossed some white plastic ties onto the kitchen counter. Brian couldn't believe only a few moments had passed since she'd shot Nathan Carter. He was unmoving on the white tile floor, blood pooling beneath him. If he was breathing, Brian couldn't discern it.

Mom said, "You don't have to use violence. We'll cooperate."

Miranda smiled brightly. "I know you will, or I'll shoot your son."

As Mom fastened Eddie's hands behind him she said, "You have to let me help Nathan. He's not part of this."

Miranda glanced down with disinterest. "He's not part of anything anymore."

Brian couldn't believe that he was nothing more than a corpse. That he'd been murdered right there in front of them, ruthlessly killed by this girl who could have been anyone's sister, anyone's classmate.

When Mom was done with Eddie, Miranda fastened her wrists behind her back. Brian's cast made it impossible to do the same to him. Miranda settled for fixing one tie around his free wrist and then through a belt loop in the back of his jeans.

"Both of you go sit on that sofa," Miranda said, waving toward the middle of the living room. "If you try something stupid, I'll shoot you through the head. Have you ever seen brain on the walls? I have. It's not pretty."

Brian and Mom sat. Miranda pushed Eddie down the hall, out of sight.

"Where's your phone?" Brian whispered, keeping an eye out for her. His own was in his room, too far away. The nearest landline was in the kitchen area, near Nathan Carter's dead body.

"It's in my purse."

He could see her paisley purse on top of the glass dining room table.

"No," Mom said. "Don't."

"I have to try," Brian said.

Sitting down had been a lot easier than standing up. With the cast and sling hampering him, and one hand fastened behind his back, he couldn't maneuver himself upright. He stopped trying when he heard Miranda's footsteps in the hall.

"He's not going anywhere," she said. She sat in the white armchair a few feet away from them and propped her feet on the glass coffee table. Out came her phone, so she could check her messages. "But you two are, in just a little while. You'll get to meet my father in person."

Mom said, "Why do you have to use a gun? We would have come with you without shooting anyone."

"I doubt it," Miranda said. "Besides which, we've had enough of sweet Uncle Henrik's double-crossing. You know how many of the diamonds were in Miami? Hardly any. He lied about those, too."

Brian's brain felt sluggish, like he'd been hit by the head when he wasn't looking. Shock, maybe. "There are diamonds in Miami?"

"There were supposed to be," Miranda said and dialed a number. She waited for someone on the other end to pick up and said, "Yes, we're here. All ready for you."

She hung up and gave them another bright smile. "I've never had a big family. Hardly any family at all, really, after my father was sent to jail for the crimes your husband committed, Hannah. I bet he never told you about those. Kept it all a secret. No more secrets now, right?"

Brian was proud of the way Mom calmly said, "I have faith in my husband."

Miranda's smile dimmed. "My father had faith in him, too. Right up until the moment Henrik had him imprisoned, took several dozen diamonds from the family vault, and fled to America."

"That's your father's version of the story," Mom said. "You need to consider both sides."

"I don't need to do anything, Hannah," snapped Miranda. "In a very short time, my father and your husband will be arriving by boat. We'll all be taking a nice trip to the Cayman Islands. Think of it as a family reunion. If everyone stays calm, then everyone will end up safe and satisfied."

"Like Nathan Carter?" Brian asked, his voice cracking.

"For millions of dollars in diamonds, I'll shoot anyone," Miranda said.

In the other room, Brian's cell phone began to ring.

CHAPTER THIRTY-FIVE

He's not answering," Denny said as Steven dug through the dirty laundry pile at the foot of his bed. "Hurry up."

"This theory of yours might be crack," Steven said.

"Just find it."

Steven unearthed the business card Lucy Mcdaniel had given him. While Denny tried to reach Brian, Steven dialed Lucy. He put it on his speakerphone.

"Hi, you've definitely reached me!" Lucy's voice said. "You do your thing after the beep does its thing, okay?"

Steven said, "Hey, this is Steven Anderson. I wanted to talk to you about that thing my dad's been ducking you about. Call me when you get this."

After he hung up, Denny said, "Notice she didn't say her name."

"Lots of people don't," Steven said, exasperated. "Look, I don't like her, but that doesn't mean I think she's in on this."

"I'm going to Brian's house," Denny said.

"He's on his way to St. Thomas."

"I'm taking the boat."

Steven began dialing. "I'll call Nathan Carter."

"I should answer my phone," Brian said.

"No need," Miranda said. "There's no one you should be talking to right now."

Her phone rang next. She watched the display screen but didn't answer. "It's your friend, the teen detective. Very handsome young man. Both of them, actually."

"If you don't answer, they'll keep calling you," Brian said. "They'll go looking for you."

"They can look all they want. They won't know how to find me."

The sky had gone dusky and dim with the setting of the sun. Palm fronds outside the patio doors see-sawed in the rising wind. Brian tried to imagine what Denny might do if he were in this situation.

Out of the corner of his eye, he saw Nathan Carter twitch.

Not a lot.

But definitely a twitch.

He needed medical attention, and fast.

Or maybe Carter was playing possum. Any minute now he might rise up like an action hero, guns blazing as he saved the day.

Brian didn't think Carter was quite that much of a superhero.

If he and Mom were going to survive this, Brian had to start thinking fast.

Miranda's phone beeped again.

"Very tiresome," she said.

Mom asked, "Is revenge really worth it, Miranda?"

Miranda leaned back in the armchair. Her gun rested in her lap, but the chances of her shooting herself seemed pretty slim.

"Revenge is always worth it. My mother and I lost our house, her job, my chances of staying in school. This is my chance for a future."

Brian said, "You're smart and beautiful. How much more of a chance do you need?"

She said, "You're very sweet, Brian. In a dorky, clueless kind of way."

She rose and went to the patio doors to look out at the dark sky and water. A few minutes later her phone rang again. This time she answered it. "Yes? All right. Don't worry about the evidence."

She turned around and said, "That was my father. They're only a mile or two away. Hannah, I hope you'll forgive me, but this really is for the best."

Miranda took out a cigarette lighter and set fire to the white curtains beside her.

❖

Denny raced the *Sleuth-hound* past Beacon Point toward Brian's house. The weather had started to turn sour—cold wind, rising waves, a smattering of rain. His phone rang and Steven said, "The line's still open, but I can't hear much."

They hadn't heard much when Carter first picked up, either—voices in the distance. Brian and his mom, maybe.

But then, her voice closer than anyone else, Lucy Mcdaniel.

"I'm two minutes away," Steven said, from behind the wheel of his truck.

"I'll beat you." Denny could already see the Vandermark house on the water. Lights shone inside, white and steady.

Steven warned, "Don't do anything stupid."

"I wouldn't," Denny said, even though he felt reckless and determined.

Three figures emerged from the house and walked down the dock. Denny didn't think they were coming to meet him specifically, which meant someone else was on the way. He didn't have a gun or any other kind of weapon. Or a plan. And what he was doing was probably the very definition of "reckless."

He pulled up alongside and cut the engine.

In the gloom he recognized Lucy with a gun and two hostages—Brian and his mother, each looking grim.

"You!" Lucy exclaimed and turned the gun his way.

"Hi," he said as confidently as he could. "My dad's on his way, with the entire police force and FBI behind him."

Brian gaped at him.

Lucy said, "You're lying. I don't hear any sirens."

"She set the house on fire!" Mrs. Vandermark said. "Nathan and Eddie are inside—"

"Shut up, Hannah," Lucy said, the gun swinging around again.

Mrs. Vandermark plowed into her, knocking her right off the dock and into the water.

At the same time her gun discharged, a shot zinging off.

"Mom!" Brian yelled as Mrs. Vandermark teetered and almost fell in herself.

Denny scrambled and grabbed Mrs. Vandermark before she could fall into the water. Once she was safe, he peered down in the black water. Lucy sputtered and splashed to the surface, her face contorted.

"I can't swim!" she yelled.

"Let her drown," Mrs. Vandermark said, which was maybe the last thing Denny expected.

"Hold on to the ladder," Denny called down to her.

A window broke behind them. Denny saw bright orange flames licking out past the shards. Lucy really had set the place on fire. Swiftly Denny used his pocket knife to start freeing Brian and Mrs. Vandermark. Steven's truck pulled into the circular drive with a squeal of brakes, and he climbed out with his cell phone in hand.

"Call nine-one-one!" Denny shouted. "The house is on fire!"

"Already on the line," Steven said, jogging toward them.

Lucy was still screeching in the water. "Get me out of here! I'll drown!"

"We have to save them," Mrs. Vandermark said to Steven. "Nathan Carter's on the kitchen floor. Eddie's in the master bedroom or bathroom."

Steven saw the fire, blanched. He sprinted toward the front door.

"Wait!" Denny yelled. Damn it. Steven couldn't just barge into a blazing house without a plan—

He heard an approaching boat, saw a light coming toward them on the water.

"That's Poul," Mrs. Vandermark said. "He's got my husband hostage."

He had guns, no doubt. And he probably wasn't alone, Denny thought, remembering the German man from Tavernier and Key West.

"Get into the boat," Denny said, pushing Brian down the dock. "We'll outrace them."

Brian said, "But Carter—"

"Steven will save him, and the fire department will be here soon," Denny said. "Go, go."

With his arm in the sling, Brian couldn't get over the edge of the boat unassisted. His mother followed him, but as Denny started the engines she leapt back onto the dock.

"Mom!" Brian said.

She only had eyes for Denny. "I'll help your brother, you help my son! Get him out of here and keep him safe."

Brian immediately exclaimed, "No, Mom, don't!"

Red lights appeared in the trees—two cruisers, maybe three. Denny made his decision. He turned the *Sleuth-hound* away from the dock.

"You can't!" Brian shouted and tried to wrestle the steering wheel from Denny's hands. "Go back!"

Something popped near Denny's ear, like a firecracker. Then a second pop.

"Get down!" Denny yelled, and pushed Brian down to the deck.

He crouched low himself, sped away from land, and hoped to hell that Steven didn't get himself killed in the burning house behind them.

CHAPTER THIRTY-SIX

Surrounded by thick smoke and shooting flames, Steven thought, *This is not the best plan I've ever had.*

But he kept low, kept crawling, using his hands to try to find what his eyes couldn't see.

"Carter!" he yelled, coughing on the bitter, hot air. "Answer me!"

He heard nothing over the whoosh and crackle of fire as it ate up the living room and ceiling.

Steven had never been in the Vandermark house before, but it had been built by the same people who'd built Jennifer O'Malley's house. High ceilings, open floor plan. The kitchen was maybe to his left. Tile under his knees and hands—that was a good sign. He was counting every time his right knee hit the floor: eleven, twelve, thirteen.

"Help!" Eddie's voice, not too far away, high with terror. "Help me!"

"Eddie! Hold on!"

The fire kept growing. Steven thought he could hear sirens from outside, but maybe that was wishful thinking. He kept moving forward, kept his hands moving. When he touched something like a tree log, he realized he'd found Carter.

Leg, knee, a splayed arm. Yes, a body. Alive or dead, too big to be Eddie, must be Carter.

"Help! I'm in the bathroom!" Eddie yelled.

Something wet under Steven's hands now. Blood.

Smoke clogged up his lungs, blinded him. A reasonable person would get out while he could. Steven wasn't reasonable. He grabbed the legs and started dragging Carter backward along the way he had come. Fifteen, fourteen, thirteen—

Carter was no lightweight. He was like a two-hundred-pound sack of concrete. Pulling him tore at the muscles in Steven's arms and back.

He's dead, said a voice in Steven's head. *Leave him. Find Eddie.*

Find your best friend.

"Help!" Fainter now, as if Eddie didn't have much strength left.

With a monstrous crack, part of the living room ceiling collapsed downward in an explosion of fiery timber and flying embers.

Fear clawed up through Steven's gut, but he kept pulling. Already he knew he was going to be too late for Carter, for Eddie, for himself. Coughing doubled him onto himself, and the spasms of his lungs made him fold over Carter's ankles.

Someone bumped into him in the thick smoke, reached for Carter with long slim arms, and started pulling the heavy body.

"Pull!" Mrs. Vandermark yelled.

Together they dragged Carter to the front door. Steven only knew they had arrived because the air got cooler, wetter. Bodies in rubbery suits appeared all around them and started helping.

Thank goodness for the Fisher Key Fire Department.

"Eddie!" he told them as someone with a helmet and big face mask lifted him to his feet. Steven couldn't tell up from down anymore, left from right, but he knew he was being taken away. He fought against it. "In the house!"

"Easy, kid," said the fireman who was holding him.

But nothing was easy anymore—not breathing, not seeing, not keeping himself conscious.

He slid into darkness thinking *I failed, failed, failed...*

❖

Pain everywhere, or everywhere that mattered. His chest, his head, his hands. Someone was talking to him, but all he could hear was Eddie screaming for help and the terrible crackle of fire eating wood and fabric. He was sure fire was still burning into him, past his skin into his bones.

"—to the ER, and we'll keep looking," someone finished saying.

Steven forced his eyes open. He was lying on the ground under a steady patter of rain. No, not rain. Spray from fire hoses aimed at the Vandermark house. Somehow Steven had ended up on an ambulance gurney with an oxygen mask over his nose.

"No hospital," he gasped and snatched the mask off. "Eddie."

A man standing close to him said, "It's okay, kid. Your friend was tied to the towel bar, but he got free and out through the bathroom window."

Sure enough, there was Eddie sitting in the ambulance. He too was wearing a mask and had a blanket slung over his shoulders, but he looked a lot better than Steven felt. Beside him was Mrs. Vandermark, watching the firemen put out the fire.

"The police found his mother and his girlfriend locked up in the trunk of the girlfriend's car, both of them fine," said the man over Steven. "Do you remember me?"

It took a second or two. "You're Agent Crown."

The FBI agent nodded. "You nearly got yourself killed in there, but good job saving Carter's life."

"He's alive?"

Agent Garcia appeared behind Crown—haggard, angry, with blood on his white shirt. "He's on his way to the E.R."

"You should go," Crown said.

Garcia shook his head. "He'd want me to nail the bastards."

A paramedic crossed the short distance between the ambulance and Steven's gurney. "We need to get you to the hospital."

"No." Steven pulled himself upright. He felt lightheaded and dehydrated, as if he'd been sitting in the sun for hours. "I need to find my brother."

The paramedics and firemen who knew Dad—and that was all of them—tried to argue with Steven. Steven refused to be persuaded. "I'm not going," he said over and over until they left him alone. Crown and Garcia helped free him of the blanket and oxygen line and gurney.

"The Coast Guard is looking for your brother's boat," Crown said. "No sign of them."

"If they're being chased, would your brother try to lay low?"

"Yeah," Steven said. "He'd hole up somewhere safe. He might not want to use the radio, but he's got his phone."

Garcia held up a broken hunk of metal. "This phone? It was on the dock. He must have dropped it."

"There's a storm warning out," Crown said. "Where would he go?"

Steven looked out at the churning waves. Lightning flashed in the west, a crack of light and sound that promised more to come.

"I need your phone," he told Crown.

When Crown gave it to him Garcia asked, "Who are you calling?"

"We need a boat," Steven said. "And I know a girl who hates me."

CHAPTER THIRTY-SEVEN

Three bullets whizzed over their heads in quick succession. Then none at all.

"Keep down!" Denny snapped as Brian started to rise beside him.

"Can you outrun them?" Brian asked.

"I'm trying," Denny said.

Lightning cracked across the sky and rain began to pelt down as Denny steered toward Whale Point and Mercy Key. He'd thought about running straight down the coast, but it seemed more likely he could lose their pursuers in the bays and coves of the offshore islands.

He had the home-field advantage, after all.

And a keen desire not to get shot.

Unfortunately, they had the disadvantage of poor visibility and worsening weather. Denny had no desire to be caught on open water in a storm.

Brian said, "They're falling behind," and he was right. The boat behind them was fast, but not as fast as the *Sleuth-hound*. The bullets stopped coming when Denny rounded the southern tip of Mercy Key. Brian cautiously stood up.

"My mom," he said, his voice cracking.

"Is fine," Denny said. "And so is my brother. We can circle back to the Coast Guard station—"

The engine began to sputter.

Denny swore and said, "They must have nicked the fuel line."

Brian asked, "Does that mean we're going to blow up?"

"No. It means we're going to run out of gas."

"What do we do?"

"We put in," Denny said.

The *Sleuth-hound* limped into Howe's Point, east of the rotted old pier that was now a navigation hazard. Denny anchored her and reached for his phone. His pocket was empty.

"Where's your phone?" he asked Brian.

"At the house. Where's yours?"

"I had it on the pier," Denny said, dismay spreading through his stomach. "I must have dropped it."

Brian shivered as the rain grew heavier. "Do you have a radio?"

"Yes, but it's open frequency. Everyone will hear us."

If it weren't for Poul and the storm, Denny would stay in the boat. But he couldn't chance it now. He crouched next to the storage locker and started shoving supplies into a knapsack.

"There's an old Civil War fort here," he told Brian. "We'll have to go ashore, use it for shelter. This here—" he held it up for Brian "—is an EPIRB. An emergency beacon. A satellite will bounce the signal to the Coast Guard."

He shoved the beacon into the backpack, made sure the anchor was secure, and fished the life jackets out from under the bench. He also pulled out a plastic bag.

"You're going to have to ditch the sling for now," he told Brian. "We'll try to keep your cast dry, but no promises."

"Do we need life jackets? How deep is it?"

"Only about four feet, but the waves are going to make it higher." Denny didn't really want to sit around and debate it, so he started undoing the sling for Brian. "We won't be in the water long."

It was easier to make that promise than keep it. Once they were over the side, the waves slammed into them like punches. He tied his and Brian's jackets together to make sure a riptide didn't suck Brian away. It physically hurt Denny to abandon the *Sleuth-hound,* but it would physically hurt more if Uncle Poul showed up and started shooting again.

Half-swimming, half-dragging each other, they fought against the push and pull of waves and undertow toward shore. A large wave slammed Denny from behind, pushing him under, smashing Brian down next. Denny felt the backpack line snap. He groped for it frantically in the underwater blackness, grazed it with his fingertips, lost it again to the water.

Sputtering back to surface he yelled, "Grab it!" but Brian didn't know what he meant, and another wave was pushing them both under again.

Denny remembered how Mom and Dad used to drill him on water safety. You can drown in a few inches of water, Dad used to say. Denny was surrounded by more than a few inches, but damn it if he was going to drown.

He pushed the backpack problem out of his mind and fought his way forward, bringing Brian with him.

They got to the sandy shoreline and collapsed there, waves still trying to grab them by the ankles. His face contorted, Brian cradled his broken arm. "What about the backpack?" he called. "Should we go back to the boat?"

Denny coughed out seawater that was making his throat and chest ache. "Too dangerous. The fort's not far—we'll come back in the morning."

Steven would immediately object to that kind of thinking, but Steven wasn't here, thanks much, and Denny's number-one job was to keep Brian safe for the foreseeable future. Denny's best flashlight had been in the backpack, but the life jacket had a smaller light tethered to it and he knew the island well enough to get them to the footpath winding away from the beach.

Once in the overgrowth and foliage, they were sheltered some from the rain, but the wind whipped branches and leaves at them and the ground was treacherous with mud.

"How far is it?" Brian asked.

"Not far. You okay?"

"Yeah."

He didn't sound okay. Denny himself probably wouldn't sound okay if he'd been held hostage and watched his house get set on fire. He didn't have anything useful to say so he kept them moving through the storm until they reached the first crumbling bricks of the old fort.

It wasn't much, as forts went. Not nearly as big as Fort Jefferson in the Dry Tortugas, and only half-built before the money ran out, but still fun to explore in good weather. Long overgrown with vines, no roof or proper floors, ammunition room walls built but never finished. A ridiculously easy place to trip and hurt yourself in, which was why Denny and Steven always found it fun.

The northwest corner of the ruins offered some limited shelter—two walls wedged together under the canopy of trees, the ground sloped enough to drain the rain. Denny got Brian seated in the driest part with the life jackets as pillows against the rough brick. Brian sat with his knees drawn up, guarding his arm.

Denny sat beside him, careful not to touch his leg or good arm. Rain drizzled down on them, but the thunder and lightning had eased off. Maybe the storm was already over, Denny thought hopefully. Or maybe another squall was coming.

Brian was very quiet and unmoving.

"Sorry if this is a crappy rescue," Denny offered.

"It's the best rescue ever," Brian said fervently, but then he was quiet again.

Denny thought on the scale of one to ten this was a negative number rescue. They were both wet, Brian was in obvious pain, the backpack with all their supplies was lost, and Denny had been a dumbass not to radio for help when he'd had the chance.

Maybe he should swim back to the *Sleuth-hound*.

But Poul Damgaard might come to them before the Coast Guard did. Poul and his gun.

"If you stop shivering, that's a bad sign," Denny said. "Hypothermia."

"Okay."

Denny used the small light to examine Brian's face and pupils. "Are you sure you're okay? Did you hit your head?"

"I'm worried about my mom, and Henrik, and your brother, and Nathan Carter—"

Denny put his hand on Brian's good arm. "Slow down before you hyperventilate."

Brian covered his face with his left hand. "I'm not good with emergencies."

"Wait until your tenth or eleventh shootout," Denny said. "It'll be a cakewalk."

"I don't know what that word means."

"Piece of cake."

Brian considered. "Chocolate cake? Lemon?"

"Whatever you want."

"With ice cream?"

Denny said, "Any flavor at all."

Brian sighed. "I didn't have dinner."

"I can catch us some fish come morning."

"You were a Boy Scout, weren't you?" Brian asked.

"Five years." Denny patted the reassuring weight of the army knife in his pocket. He was already planning how he could catch a fish and cook it, if they dared risk a campfire. "Then we started karate classes in Key West and something had to give."

Another squall rolled over them—harder rain, colder. Denny began to calculate the odds of hypothermia. Their soaking wet clothes weren't a good start. The drum of water on the bricks and trees made talk impossible, so he scooted a few inches closer to Brian and tried to think positive thoughts.

Steven's fine.

The *Sleuth-hound* is fine.

Nathan Carter isn't dead.

The Coast Guard will find the beacon.

We won't be dead by then.

He hunkered down to wait out the storm.

CHAPTER THIRTY-EIGHT

Agent Crown looked like he was trying hard not to vomit. Garcia didn't look much better. Neither of them suggested that they stop searching, but the storm was getting worse with the passing hours, and Steven knew he was endangering everyone.

Still, he couldn't stop—not with Denny out there somewhere on the dark ocean. He kept the *Docket* moving across the waves.

Standing beside him in the covered flybridge, wrapped in a big yellow raincoat, Kelsey said, "Think like your brother. Wouldn't he have put in somewhere nice and dry?"

He'd objected to her coming along, but she said he had no choice if he wanted to use her father's boat. It wasn't worth arguing over. And he was kind of glad, maybe, to have her along, even if she was still mad at him over Jennifer O'Malley.

The boat heaved on the waves. Visibility sucked. He was relying on the navigation gear and his own experience to keep them from running ashore on one of the keys or reefs. His head and chest ached from the smoke inhalation earlier, and the skin on his hands was pink and tight.

"Denny would have called the Coast Guard if he was safe," Steven said.

Garcia was in charge of monitoring the radio. Crown was in charge of staying on his own two feet. Kelsey had announced she would make coffee for all of them, but the seas were too rough to risk boiling water.

Kelsey put her hand on Steven's shoulder and kneaded his tight muscles. "You can't help him if we run aground."

Steven glared through the plastic window at the wind-tossed ocean and flickering skies. He knew what Denny would say—put ashore, stay alive. His dad would say the same thing.

The boat heaved again.

"Damn it," he said and turned toward the Coast Guard station.

The station captain, Dermot Flaherty, was a friend of Dad's. He eyed the first-degree burns on Steven's arms and face and said, critically, "Go lie down in my office before you fall down."

"But I want to—"

"Right now," Captain Flaherty said. "There's a cot there with your name on it."

Steven obeyed, but he didn't sleep. Instead, he listened to the murmur of voices that drifted under the door and tried to use twin telepathy to find Denny. He didn't actually believe in telepathy— neither of them did—but he'd take anything he could get on this miserable night.

Maybe he did fall asleep, just a little, because when he blinked his eyes the sun had started to rise and Kelsey was curled up in Captain Flaherty's armchair, sleeping under someone's uniform coat.

He let her sleep and went in search of the Command Center, where the crew on duty was watching screens and monitoring communications. Captain Flaherty was drinking from a coffee mug the size of a thermos.

"Your parents are on their way back from Tallahassee," Flaherty said. "They're pretty worried."

Steven was worried too, but he didn't feel like saying it aloud.

"Sir, we think we've found it," said one of the petty officers nearby. "The EPIRB matches for Dennis Anderson and the *Sleuth-hound*."

Steven instantly moved to study the display. Mercy Key, Whale Island, and Longman's Key formed an irregular line to Fisher Key's east. The blinking light for the beacon was off Longman's Key.

"We thought we had a fix on it a half hour ago," Captain Flaherty said, his hand heavy on Steven's shoulder. "The signal's been weak and intermittent, though. It looks like she's drifting south. A boat's already on the way."

Steven went to round up Kelsey and then Crown and Garcia, who were napping in a conference room. They were halfway to Longman's Key when the patrol boat radioed in they'd found the beacon afloat, no sign of the *Sleuth-hound*.

"It doesn't mean they sank," Kelsey said, squeezing Steven's hand.

"Your brother's fine," Garcia added, looking hollow-eyed and gray in the morning sun. Steven knew he was still worried about Carter, who at last word was in surgery in Tavernier.

Crown added in, "He's a resourceful kid."

They all meant well, but Steven didn't believe them. The *Sleuth-hound*'s EPIRB was designed to automatically broadcast when submerged. If the beacon was in the water, the boat was probably submerged as well.

With his brother and Brian aboard.

Drowned and dead at the bottom of the ocean.

CHAPTER THIRTY-NINE

"Talk to me," Brian said.

The rain would stop for short periods, then burst down on them again as more storm clouds passed overhead.

Denny said, "You should get some sleep."

"Talk me to sleep. I need something—something other than what's in my head."

So Denny talked. Brian listened to stories about the Boy Scouts, and about how Denny and Steven started camping on their own at age thirteen.

"Dad dropped us off right on this island. We pitched a tent, caught our own dinner, thought we were real men. Afterward we found out he only anchored out of sight. But that tent was the best birthday present ever."

Brian smiled, or thought he did. His eyes were closed as he drifted along the shores of exhaustion and discomfort.

Denny kept talking. About how he and Steven had earned Boy Scout merit badges in Crime Prevention after solving their first mystery at age twelve. About his dad, who'd played football at the University of Miami but would never let his sons play, because he thought they were already soft in the head and didn't need more brain injuries.

Brian was pretty sure that was a joke.

Denny kept talking. The steady, comfortable sound helped drown out the horrible little voice inside that kept saying *Nathan Carter's dead, Mom's in danger.*

"And I knew right after talking to him that I wanted to be in the Coast Guard," Denny was saying. Brian wasn't sure how they had gotten onto this topic, but he didn't open his eyes to ask. Denny continued, "No other options. But it's kind of depressing because I don't want to be part of an organization that discriminates. There was this officer we knew over at the Coast Guard station, Lieutenant Murphy. Saved three people in a plane crash. He was gay and everyone knew it. Nobody cared. Then he was transferred north and his new commanding officer had him discharged for being seen in a gay bar. What kind of crap is that?"

Brian wanted to say that it was the kind of crap that was unfortunately common, but exhaustion dragged him down into a black sea of nothingness.

Only a few minutes had passed, at best, before he realized he was on fire. Burning, the flames licking up his clothes and toward his face—

"Easy, easy!" Denny said, as Brian flailed awake. Before them was a tiny fire, nothing more than a handful of twigs but blessedly warm. The sky was still dark behind Denny.

"Sun's coming up soon," Denny said.

Brian said thickly, "I don't see it." Then, "Where'd you get the fire?"

"I made it." Denny sounded amused. "Merit badge, remember?"

Brian moved closer to the warmth. As the sun came up he saw more of the fort around them. Not so much a fort but lots of bricks and greenery, maybe. Denny offered to catch some lizards to snack on, or unearth some grubs, but Brian put a stop to that talk.

"I'll wait for real food."

"It is real food," Denny said, but he didn't insist.

They hiked back to the beach past ferns and trees that looked impenetrable in the daylight. Brian was surprised Denny had even found the path last night. After a half mile or so they were stepping out onto the beach, where the storm tides had left behind new driftwood and a fine littering of sea plants. The *Sleuth-hound* was moored offshore, exactly where they had left her.

Denny abruptly pulled Brian back into the brush.

"What?" Brian hissed, his arm in agony from the sudden jostling.

"Look beyond her," Denny said.

A forty-foot cabin cruiser was anchored just beyond the *Sleuth-hound.* A sleek boat, modern, no sign of life.

"Your uncle found us," Denny muttered. "Come on."

Denny went off the path into the trees, choosing his footing carefully. Brian felt clumsy and awkward as he followed. They had shared some gathered rainwater back at the fort, but Brian was still thirsty, and starving, and in dire need of caffeine and his painkillers both.

He didn't complain, though. If Denny didn't complain, Brian wouldn't either.

They reached the south end of the island several minutes later. No sandy beaches here, just mangroves giving way to the sea and the sight of another key not too far away.

"That's Bardet Key," Denny said. "Steven and I inherited an old fishing shack there from a friend of my mom's. I'm pretty sure we left a flare gun there last trip over."

Brian studied the distance with dismay. "I can't swim that far."

"No," Denny said steadily. "But I can."

Brian blinked at him. "What? No! You can't leave me."

"Once I fire the flare, Steven will see it." Denny sounded absolutely sure that his brother was out there searching for them. Brian wondered what it was like to have such faith in someone. "It also might scare your uncle off when he realizes help is coming."

"Or make him go after you," Brian protested.

The breeze blew Denny's hair back from his forehead. He looked very handsome against the backdrop of the sea, like a male model posing for a magazine. Well, a rumpled and tired male model who hadn't gotten any sleep and was just as hungry as Brian was.

Denny pulled off his shoes and handed them to Brian. "It's only a mile or so. I can swim it in about a half-hour. Your job is to stay hidden, stay out of sight. Don't let your uncle lure you out. Can you do that?"

"No," Brian said. "I need you here."

For a moment, the determination on Denny's face flickered. Brian knew then that Denny wanted to stay with him, but was doing the one thing he thought would save them both.

Brian said, "Go. Be safe. Don't get eaten by sharks."

Denny nodded and waded into the surf, leaving Brian behind.

❖

Denny hadn't been lying when he said he could swim a mile in a half-hour. Usually less, in fact. He'd timed himself more than once in a swimming pool. The ocean was no pool, however. As he set off with a steady stroke the push and pull of the ocean reminded him how easily he could be pulled off course, tugged toward or away from Bardet Key. The hollowness in his stomach reminded him that he hadn't eaten anything substantial since lunch yesterday. He should have dug up some grubs during the long dark hours of the night.

Still, hunger or not, he could do this.

He kept swimming.

The water was warm but choppy. He wished Brian hadn't mentioned sharks. Stretch his arm, scoop water, breathe, kick from the thighs—he knew the rhythm, had performed it for years, but urgency made him clumsy and he forced himself to slow down.

Alternate your strokes, he heard Steven say, as surely as if his twin was right there with him. His annoying, irritating, know-it-all twin, who had better not be dead right now.

After several minutes Denny rolled over and did the backstroke. Easier that way, but the sun stung the salt on his face. He turned into a sidestroke. Steady. Keep breathing.

When he stopped to figure out his speed and course, he saw that the current was pulling him east. He'd have to swim diagonally instead of straight. Danny glanced back to Mercy Key, but it had retreated into a smudge of green and there was no sign of Brian at all.

Brave, steadfast Brian, who hadn't complained at all about this mess Denny had dragged him into.

He swam for several more minutes, trying to stay focused. Stretch, scoop, breathe, kick. He was alone under the bright, scorching sun, pale blue above and cobalt blue below, a puny human in a vast sea of sharks, jellyfish, and other hazards.

Best not to think about that now.

He imagined he was swimming at the Coast Guard Academy, showing off for all those pale northern kids.

He imagined himself as Nathan Carter, vagabond hunk, swimming around the keys at night in his tight swimming trunks. Had it only been a week since *The Tempest* blew up, setting all this craziness in motion?

Without warning, a fierce cramp grabbed his right calf and exploded in agonizing pain. The shock of it made Denny swallow a mouthful of seawater and start to sink.

Just like that, he was drowning.

CHAPTER FORTY

Brian watched Denny swim away until he was just a vanishing dot. He shaded his eyes against the sun and stared a little longer.

Don't get killed, he thought. *Come back to me.*

Finally, he retreated into the thick interior of Mercy Key and tried to keep himself hidden.

Moving as quietly as possible, swatting off flies, he tried to imagine a happy future: himself at MIT come fall, the big campus with its mix of old and new buildings, the Charles River filled with college men rowing boats. All those handsome and smart boys he'd meet. Everything he'd been planning for since Mom and Henrik dragged him down to Fisher Key.

Was there room for Denny in that picture? Did Denny want there to be?

Sure, Denny could drive up from New London. Bed down in Brian's dorm room, or they could rent a hotel room. Would he want to? He might prefer his military friends, the academy itself, never letting himself break free of the prison he kept himself in.

A voice rang out through the trees.

"Brian! Brian, answer me!"

Henrik.

Brian froze.

"Brian?" Henrik sounded more desperate, his accent heavy. "You have to come out, son. It's time to meet your uncle."

He stayed silent. Henrik had put them all in jeopardy by refusing to disclose his past—a past that seemed pretty shady. Poul's daughter had shot Nathan Carter and set fire to the house. The more Brian thought about it, the more he suspected they were a family of lunatics.

But Henrik was still his stepfather, the man who'd been part of his family for five years. He was the man that Mom loved. Brian guessed he loved him, too. Right now he couldn't tell.

Could he let him be hurt?

"Brian, please!" Henrik sounded closer now. "You have to help me out here. They just want to talk to you."

Not enough time had passed for Denny to get to Bardet Key. That was the most important thing right now.

Brian kept moving, kept silent, and promised himself that rescue would arrive soon.

The blue waters of the Atlantic shimmered all around him as Denny sank. After a few seconds of incoherent pain and near-panic, he pulled his cramped leg close and kicked upward with his good leg. He broke the surface with violent coughs.

The pain ripped and ripped at his leg, nearly made him sink again. He tried rotating his foot. That helped a little. He wheezed past the water clogging his throat and tried to drag air in through his nose. Black spots blocked his view of the sky and the sound of his own frantic heartbeat drowned out everything else.

What if he drowned out here? They might never even find his body. For the rest of their lives, Steven and his parents would never know what had happened.

Not going to drown, he told himself fiercely.

After several chancy minutes he was able to knead the knot out of his calf. His chest and throat ached, but he could breathe normally. When he looked for Bardet Key he saw that he'd been pulled eastward again, even more off course than before.

No use complaining about it.

He started swimming again. Sidestroke and backstroke, mostly. Arms and legs slicing through the waves. Seawater sloshed around in his stomach and he stopped once to vomit. Pain lingered in his cramped calf. He kept going anyway. No way was he never going to see his family again.

No way was he going to die a virgin.

He concentrated on Brian, and the way his hair flopped around, and his dorky glasses. About all the books he read and the way he stuck up for Christopher even when he didn't deserve it. About the kiss in Mom's office. About sitting next to him in the fort all night, afraid to hold him or touch him in any way that might be considered sexual.

For the first time, Denny realized how immensely screwed up his whole denial thing was.

His arms hit something hard. Confused, he rolled onto his stomach. He'd reached the shallows of Bardet Key. He dragged himself upright, staggered into the frothy surf, and went down to his knees in the sand in front of a palm tree.

For a long moment he breathed deeply and willed away the shakiness in his arms and legs.

Then he forced himself to his feet and went looking for that flare gun.

❖

Something white streaked upward from Bardet Key.

"Look!" Kelsey shouted.

The tight knot of fear that had been coiled in Steven's stomach undid itself.

"I'll be damned," Crown said. "Your brother must have nine lives."

Garcia wasn't convinced. "It might not be him."

Steven had no doubts. He turned the boat and steered toward the fishing shack Uncle Rick used to keep. Denny was on the beach there, alive but alone. Steven pulled Mr. Carlson's boat as close to shore as he could and turned the helm over to Kelsey. Denny limped down into the water and Steven met him halfway.

They eyed each other critically.

"You're limping," Steven said.

"You're burnt," Denny responded.

Crown leaned over the boat. "You okay, kid?"

"Fine," Denny said. "Brian needs help. He's over on Mercy Key and his uncle's there, too."

They hauled Denny onto the *Docket*. Kelsey got him some water and cheese from the galley. On the flybridge, Steven filled him in on the fire and Nathan Carter. Crown was busy on the radio, letting the Coast Guard know Denny had been rescued and directing the police toward Mercy Key.

By the time they reached the island, two police boats and the Coast Guard were on the horizon. Poul Damgaard's boat was still anchored by the *Sleuth-hound*. No one was aboard, which meant they were on land chasing Brian.

Crown said, "You kids stay here."

Garcia added, "This is FBI business now."

"But we can't—" Denny started to argue.

Steven stopped him with a hand on his arm. "No, he's right. If the bad guys circle back around to here, someone's got to stop them."

Crown and Garcia exchanged looks.

"All right, Steven, you come with me," Garcia said. "Denny, you stay here with my partner."

"Why me?" Denny asked indignantly.

"Limping," Steven reminded him.

Denny stood to prove he was fine, but his leg was obviously cramping up again.

Crown asked, "And why am I staying behind?"

"Because of Nathan," Garcia said grimly.

"No stunts," Crown said sternly. "This isn't about revenge."

Garcia checked his weapon. "I don't know what you're talking about."

Kelsey had observed the conversations without comment, but now she said, "Steven, be careful."

"I'm always careful." He followed Garcia into the water and onto dry land.

CHAPTER FORTY-ONE

Brian had secreted himself in dense greenery near the old fort. He tried to make himself as still and quiet as possible. The plan worked until something dark and slithery crawled across his foot. He panicked, scrambled away, and made a lot more noise than he should have. Someone shouted out in Danish. Brian ran as best he could past thorny vines that reached for him, grabbed him—

A pair of hands caught his shoulders and slammed him against one of the fort's old brick walls. Pain radiated down his broken arm and he gasped.

Agent Prosper from Key West—Poul Damgaard—gave him a sour, triumphant look.

"Brian," he said. "My dear nephew. We've been looking for you. Where's your friend?"

Brian tried not to squirm against the rough bricks. "Who? I came here alone."

Poul shook his head. "You wouldn't know how to steer a boat in a bathtub."

Anger flared in Brian. "How would you know?"

"I know all about you. You think I came unprepared? Your school records, your shopping habits, your disgusting fondness for other boys—all this I know."

Brian should have been intimidated. Maybe he'd been hanging around Denny too long, however, because instead he lifted his chin and said, "Then you'd better know that the police are on their way."

"Doubtful," Poul said.

He turned his head over his shoulder and shouted out in Danish. Two men emerged from the thickets—Henrik, looking disheveled with two days of beard stubble, and the German from Key West. The German had a pistol wedged into Henrik's side.

Henrik's helpless gaze settled on Brian. "Are you okay?"

"Yeah," Brian ground out. "This is your brother?"

"Yes."

"Your family sucks," Brian said.

Poul grabbed him by the scruff of his shirt and shoved him down to his knees. "Careful, boy."

"I'm sorry for all the problems this has caused," Henrik said.

"Problems?" Brian squeaked out. He hated how high his voice sounded. He hated that he was kneeling on the ground, maybe about to be killed. "She set fire to the house! She killed Nathan Carter!"

Henrik said, "You promised, Poul! No killing."

"Miranda did what she had to do," Poul said smugly. "She's my best child. She deserves to inherit the fortune our grandfathers started for us."

"She's in jail," Brian said. "I hope she rots there."

Poul cuffed the back of his head hard enough to make Brian's eyes water.

The German said something short and curt.

"I haven't forgotten," Poul said snippishly. "Where's your friend? The sheriff's son. The Coast Guard has been on the radio all night about you two."

Sunlight through the trees dazzled Brian's eyes. He felt flushed and powerful with the realization that yes, they could kill him, but they could only kill him once. At least Denny would be safe.

"I told you. I came alone," he said.

The German shoved Henrik to his knees and put the pistol to the back of his head.

"No!" Henrik yelled. "Please!"

The powerfulness that Brian had been feeling abruptly fled, leaving behind ice water in his veins. "Stop!"

Poul held up a forestalling hand. "Tell me, then. Where's your friend?"

"You don't need him," Brian insisted. "He doesn't know anything."

Something hard nuzzled the back of Brian's head. He knew that Poul's gun was now wedged against it. *This is it,* he thought. *I'm dead now.*

"Please, Poul." Henrik was crying now. Crying for Brian. "Don't do this. I made mistakes, you made mistakes, but don't let your hatred for me destroy an innocent boy."

Poul said, "This has never been about hatred, Henrik. Only justice. I gave you many chances to right your wrongs. To make amends for everything you stole from me and my loved ones. Last chance, boy. Where is the sheriff's son?"

"Right here," Denny said, stepping out over one of the low crumbled walls. He looked confident and calm, his hands in the air, his gaze only on Poul. "I'm right here. You don't have to hurt anyone."

Brian wanted to sag with relief.

But then he realized this was not Denny. The clothes were different, sure, but there were subtle differences, as well—the hair, the stance, the way he held his head.

"Come on, then," Poul said, grabbing Brian and hauling him to his feet. He tucked his gun into his belt. "We have diamonds to go find."

Brian's legs were shaky. He didn't understand what was going on. If this was Steven, where was Denny?

The German man pulled Henrik up from his knees. Brian didn't see what happened next, but heard a solid thunking noise and then turned to see the German sagging to his knees, a hunk of coral falling from his shoulder to the ground.

"FBI, freeze!" yelled Agent Garcia from atop one of the fort's few solid walls. He had a gun in his hand, and another chunk of coral waiting to drop down on them.

Poul went for his gun.

Steven tackled him.

Brian was knocked aside by the fracas. He landed hard on the ground, his broken arm bursting into white-hot agony.

Then a gun went off, so loud it nearly deafened him, and Brian saw only black.

❖

The gunshot had Denny rearing to his feet.

"Sit down before I handcuff you to the railing," Crown said. He immediately negated the threat by clambering over the side of the *Docket*. "If my idiot partner gets himself killed, I'll kill him again for good measure."

Denny vowed the same about Steven.

The Coast Guard and police boats arrived and a helicopter closed in from the west. Kelsey looked impressed. Denny was only worried about Steven and Brian. He followed Crown into the water. Hot pain like a fire poker stabbed into his calf, but he made it to the sand just as Steven emerged from the brush.

With Steven were Brian and Henrik Vandermark.

"Bad guy needs a doctor," Steven announced. "Your partner says take your time."

Crown muttered, "I bet he does."

Steven looked as invincible as ever. Brian had one hand covering his left ear, his cast was cracked, and his expression glazed.

Denny touched Brian's good arm. "Are you okay?"

"Half-deaf," was Brian's reply. "What about you?"

Denny grinned. "I had a nice swim."

Brian smiled back at him. For a moment, it was just the two of them, the only important people in the world, despite the Coast Guard officers and policemen wading ashore. Denny felt elated, overjoyed, stupendously relieved.

And Brian must have felt the same, because he leaned forward and kissed Denny. No chaste, friendly kiss, either—this was hot and strong and smack-dab on the mouth, like a lightning bolt on a summer day, so passionate that Denny might have made a soft noise of surrender before he recovered his senses and jerked away.

"Sorry," Brian said, but his expression didn't show regret.

Steven cleared his throat. "I didn't see that coming."

Denny was sure everyone was staring at him.

All these men who worked with or knew his Dad.

"Forget it," Denny said, his face burning, and he went back out into the water to claim his boat.

CHAPTER FORTY-TWO

Denny slept for a whole day, exhausted. When he finally woke up, Mom fussed over him and Dad said he'd done well. Newspapers, TV people, and bloggers were all trying to reach him, but he agreed only to talk to Janet Hogan, because he owed her.

No one said anything about the public and very embarrassing kiss.

Brian and his mother hadn't left Fisher Key, although their house was uninhabitable. They moved into a rental house near the Key West resort. Denny only knew that because Mom knew the rental agent. Meanwhile, Poul Damgaard and his daughter were in jail, and Henrik Vandermark was under investigation for fraud and other crimes by the FBI and Interpol.

"That computer hard drive from the SUV was full of financial records and incriminating evidence," Steven explained. "Poul was using it for blackmail."

Denny waited for Brian to call him at home or at the Bookmine, but there was only silence.

"You could call him," Steven suggested.

"He kissed me in front of a dozen witnesses."

"Heat of the moment! No one's going to call the Coast Guard and report you before you even start."

It felt like a weird kind of stalemate, but maybe that was too generous a word. Denny had seen the hurt on Brian's face on the sunlit beach of Mercy Key. You don't kiss a guy like that and expect him to say, "Forget it."

But Brian had given him no choice. What did he think Denny would do?

He wasn't thinking, a voice said inside Denny. *He was just happy to see you.*

Not for the first time, Denny pondered his own cowardice.

Caught up on his sleep, his leg all better, Denny still felt miserable. He moped around the house, barely ambitious enough to change the TV channel every couple of hours.

"If you don't snap out of it, I'm going to beat you," Steven threatened one night. They were in bed, the air-conditioner pumping out lukewarm air again, and Denny hated the rattle so much that he wanted to just push the unit out the window.

"I'm going outside to sleep," Denny said.

He grabbed his pillow and a sheet and went outside, where the breeze made the air marginally cooler. Long ago they'd erected twin hammocks down by the water. Denny climbed into one and stared up at the white stars. A moment later, Steven got into his own hammock.

"I mean it," Steven said. "Snap out of it."

"Your bedside manner sucks."

"You're not sick. You're sulking."

Denny wanted to throw something hard at him, but his only ammunition was his pillow. He kept that tucked under his head.

Steven said, "Honestly. Go over and pound on his door and apologize."

"He's the one who kissed me! In front of a dozen witnesses. It kind of ruins my 'stay in the closet' scheme."

"It's a sucky scheme."

"You want me to ditch the academy?"

"There are lots of gay people in the Coast Guard. Why do you have to be the only one who can't have sex?"

"Sex, or a relationship?" Denny challenged.

"You know what I mean."

"I'd know what you mean if you actually got back together with Kelsey," Denny said.

"She's still mad at me."

"So make it up to her."

Steven said nothing.

Denny listened to the water washing in and out. The sky above them stretched away and away, across the universe. He wanted to float up into it but was too tied down, too heavy for flight.

"Mom and Dad would die if they find out," he finally said.

"Says who?"

Denny heaved a theatrical sigh. "You know what? You're so big on the truth, I'll make you a deal. When you tell them the truth about SEAL training, I'll tell them that I like to kiss boys. We'll ruin their whole summer all at once."

Steven didn't answer.

The next morning Denny woke with the sun in his face. He blinked at the blue-green ocean and cloudless sky. The smell of bacon wafted from the house. When Denny got to the kitchen, Dad was cooking. Dad never cooked. Mom was wrapped in her bright orange and yellow bathrobe, reading the newspaper. Steven was wet with sweat, just in from his run.

"Morning, sweetie," Mom said.

Dad asked, "Hungry, kiddo?"

"Yeah." Denny slumped into a chair and yawned. "I could eat a horse."

Steven dropped into the chair across the table. "Mom, Dad, I didn't get into boot camp in September. I lied about SEAL training because I couldn't admit I'd failed the color test. But I'm working on getting a waiver."

Mom lowered her coffee cup and stared at him.

Dad lifted his spatula and stared at him.

Steven said, "Now Denny wants to tell you something, too."

Denny could have murdered him right there with a butter knife.

Instead of fratricide, he swallowed past a lump of panic and said, "Mom, Dad, it's come to my attention that maybe I don't like girls. The way I like boys. If you know what that means."

He dared a glance at Mom. She had a puzzled look on her face, as if she couldn't decide if they were joking or not.

Dad was frozen in place.

"I think the bacon's burning," Steven said quietly.

Slowly, Dad turned off the stove. "I think this family has a whole lot to talk about."

❖

Which was how they both ended up grounded for a week—Steven for lying, Denny for helping him keep the lie going.

As for the gay stuff?

"We're both college-educated professionals," Mom said. "I can't exactly say we're surprised."

Dad added, "It's not going to be easy for you, being gay and in the military. But what did you think? We were going to hate you? Kick you out?"

Denny's face burned as he said, "It happens to other people."

"It doesn't happen around here," Dad said and gave him a hug.

So now his parents knew, and the world kept spinning. The sun rose and set on schedule, Steven continued to stink up the bathroom with obnoxious smells, and Denny had to think hard about his future.

"Should I still go into the Coast Guard?" he asked his parents.

Mom asked, "Any reason you shouldn't?"

Dad said, "Good reasons, that is. Not some rules in Washington from politicians who've never served a day in their lives."

Denny loved his parents.

Today, Friday, was his first day back to work since the rescue on Mercy Key. Sean and Robin both wanted to know all the gritty details. To save himself from an interrogation, Denny holed himself up in the back and started putting the music section in alphabetical order. He was sorting through a dozen books about The Beatles when Mom fluttered into sight in her green and orange dress.

"There's a customer out front with some books to sell," she said. "Will you handle it?"

"Sean knows how," Denny protested.

"These are rare books. I think you'd better do it."

He trudged out front. Brian was standing at the side counter, his arm in a new cast, with a cardboard box of books that smelled like smoke and ash.

"I don't think these are worth much," Brian said, his face inscrutable. "But I wanted to salvage what I could."

Denny touched the leathery covers of the books Brian loved.

"I think they're priceless," Denny said. "Can we talk?"

"Talk about what?"'

"About me being an idiot."

The corner of Brian's mouth quirked. "Are you really an idiot?"

"And then we could go to dinner," Denny said.

Someone made a happy noise at the cash register. That was Sean, staring at them with a goofy smile while he nudged Robin to pay attention. Denny ignored both of them.

"Dinner as in…" Brian didn't finish.

"Dinner as in a date." Denny's hands had gone clammy, but he wasn't going to stop now. "A date, as in two people who like each other, and the one who's been an idiot gets to apologize some more and maybe make amends."

Brian's expression relaxed. "Yeah. That sounds like a good idea."

Denny smiled. And then he kissed Brian, hard and happy, totally ignoring the loud clapping from Robin and Sean.

❖

Ninety-five. Ninety-six. Ninety-seven.

"I think he's going to do it." That was Garcia, sounding amused.

Ninety-eight.

Carter croaked out, "I never doubted it."

Ninety-nine. One hundred. Steven did an extra push-up for good measure before sitting on the hard floor of Carter's hospital room. He tried very hard to look like he wasn't about to pass out.

Carter was sitting up in bed, still hooked up to an array of tubes and liquids but far from dead. Garcia, sitting beside him, applauded for Steven.

"Great job, kid," Garcia said.

Carter fumbled for a drinking cup with a straw in it. "They were okay."

"Okay!" Steven said indignantly. "Those were awesome."

Garcia retrieved the cup from the bedside tray and held it for Carter. "Don't let him fool you. Under all those painkillers, he's very impressed."

Carter gave Garcia an obscene gesture. Obscene, but fond.

"Will you help me get a waiver?" Steven asked.

"Already put in a good word," Carter said. "My uncle's working on it."

"Your uncle?"

"Head of the Bureau of Medicine," Garcia explained. "He didn't tell you?"

"No. He didn't tell me."

Carter yawned. "Not the head. Second-in-charge."

"Very high up," Garcia amended.

"Your dad visited yesterday," Carter said, shifting slightly against his pillows. "He said you finally confessed about failing the vision test. We agreed that you're stubborn and egotistical, and you need to learn to stop running into burning buildings."

"And throwing yourself at men with guns," Garcia added.

"You're going to make a hell of a SEAL," Carter said. "Thanks for saving my life."

Garcia reached out and touched Carter's face. "Thanks from both of us."

Steven decided to leave before kissing commenced. At the doorway he said, "Really high up in the Bureau of Medicine?"

"Big admiral," Garcia said.

"Keep practicing your push-ups," Carter said.

On his way through the lobby Steven saw Kelsey talking on her phone by the glass windows with her back toward him. He stopped, surprised. She'd done him a huge favor, but things were still awkward between them. He'd apologized. She said she understood. But that didn't mean they were back together. He didn't actually know where they stood—if he should call her, if she'd go out with him, if he should just buy a copy of that stupid book.

"Hey," he said, stepping up behind her.

The girl turned. Her eyes were green, and she had a pierced eyebrow. "Yes?"

Steven backed away, flushing. "Sorry. My mistake."

As he crossed the parking lot he decided he'd call Kelsey on the drive back down to Fisher Key. Bring her flowers, maybe some chocolates. He'd tell Jennifer that he couldn't see her again. Meanwhile he'd wait for the waiver and amp up his exercise schedule. He would not lie to his parents or anyone else. He could see it now: a quiet, uneventful summer full of fishing, kayaking, and not looking for trouble.

But life on Fisher Key was never dull, and for Steven and Denny, this summer was going to be the most exciting and dangerous one of all...

The End

Additional Information

The United States Coast Guard Academy is in New London, CT. To be accepted for study, students have to do well in high school, achieve high SAT scores, submit original essays, pass a physical fitness exam, and have evaluations from math, English, and physical fitness teachers. Each year, more than two thousand students apply for admission. Only four hundred will be accepted, and half will graduate and serve five years of obligatory military service.

There are many ways to become a Navy SEAL, and most begin with a Physical Screening Test (PST). This test includes push-ups, sit-ups, pull-ups, swimming, and running 1.5 miles in less than 11 minutes. Candidates must also score well on the ASVAB (Armed Services Vocational Aptitude Battery) test, which is offered to all high school students, and have a clean criminal record. SEAL training is extremely arduous and requires enormous mental and physical strength.

Keep reading for a special preview of *The Secret of Othello,*
Book 2 of the Fisher Key Adventures by Sam Cameron,
coming in 2012.

FROM THE SECRET OF OTHELLO

Furious that Denny was not answering his phone, Steven decided to walk home. It wasn't far—nothing on Fisher Key was far—but it was very late, he was tired, and his knee was still stiff from the fight. This side of the island didn't have street lights, but the moon was bright. All he had to do was follow South Road around the point toward the marina, crossing Jeffers Bridge along the way.

Every few minutes he dialed Denny and left a snarky message.

"I hope you're having a really good time with your boyfriend and my truck," he said.

And then, "Wish I had back the truck I pay for with my own money every month."

And also, "Remember my truck? You're never borrowing it again for the rest of your life, got it?"

No houses along here, just mangroves and marsh and the occasional whoosh of a car on the nearby Overseas Highway. Stars glittered overhead and waves washed up against the thin strip of shoreline. Steven didn't know if he could ever live in a city, with traffic and pollution and people jammed together in high-rises. He wasn't even sure what to expect on a military base, only what he'd read or watched in movies—barracks, chow halls, reveille every morning, everything rigid and orderly. No palm trees or salty breezes, no chirp of a million insects on the road.

Jeffers Bridge was a concrete stretch that crossed over one of the largest inlets on the island. As Steven started across, headlights came up behind him and turned his silhouette into a long shadow. He turned and shielded his eyes against the glare. At first he thought it was Denny catching up with him, but the engine noise wasn't quite right. Maybe it was another local and he could hitch a ride—

The engine revved.

The headlights switched to high beams. The driver gunned straight toward him.

Steven started to run.

But even as he sprinted, he knew he wasn't going to make it. The bridge was too long, his knee too stiff, and the truck or SUV too fast. In just a few seconds, Steven was going to be a large splat of road kill. Wouldn't that suck rotten eggs? His entire life, over before he even got to the good parts.

He veered toward the bridge railing, got his hands on the rusty metal, and swung himself over the side. For a few brief seconds there was only the panic of being in mid-air and falling helplessly, a total victim of gravity. Then he hit the warm water, sank over his head, and kicked to the surface. The outgoing current dragged him under the bridge. He grabbed for a pylon and clung tight, though sea moss made it slippery.

Above him, brakes screeched. Steven listened hard, but the concrete muffled other noises. A few seconds later, the beam from a flashlight sliced down into the water just a few feet away and a man's voice yelled, "Nice try, kid! Get back up here!"

Steven kept silent.

The white beam swung closer.

The man said, "Show yourself and say hi to your brother, or I'll put this bullet right through his head."

About the Author

A Navy veteran, Sam Cameron spent several years serving in the Pacific and along the Atlantic coast. Her transgender, romance, and science fiction stories have been recognized for their wit, inventiveness, and passion. She holds an MFA in Creative Writing and currently teaches college in Florida.

Soliloquy Titles From Bold Strokes Books

Mystery of the Tempest: A Fisher Key Adventure by Sam Cameron. Twin brothers Denny and Steven Anderson love helping people and fighting crime alongside their sheriff dad on sundrenched Fisher Key, Florida, but Denny doesn't dare tell anyone he's gay, and Steven has secrets of his own to keep. (978-1-60282-579-6)

Swimming to Chicago by David-Matthew Barnes. As the lives of the adults around them unravel, high school students Alex and Robby form an unbreakable bond, vowing to do anything to stay together—even if it means leaving everything behind. (978-1-60282-572-7)

Speaking Out edited by Steve Berman. Inspiring stories written for and about LGBT and Q teens of overcoming adversity (against intolerance and homophobia) and experiencing life after "coming out." (978-1-60282-566-6)

365 Days by K.E. Payne. Life sucks when you're seventeen years old and confused about your sexuality, and the girl of your dreams doesn't even know you exist. Then in walks sexy new emo girl, Hannah Harrison. Clemmie Atkins has exactly 365 days to discover herself, and she's going to have a blast doing it! (978-1-60282-540-6)

Cursebusters! by Julie Smith. Budding-psychic Reeno is the most accomplished teenage burglar in California, but one tiny screw-up and poof!—she's sentenced to Bad Girl School. And that isn't even her worst problem. Her sister Haley's dying of an illness no one can diagnose, and now she can't even help. (978-1-60282-559-8)

Who I Am by M.L. Rice. Devin Kelly's senior year is a disaster. She's in a new school in a new town, and the school bully is making her life miserable—but then she meets his sister Melanie and realizes her feelings for her are more than platonic. (978-1-60282-231-3)

Sleeping Angel by Greg Herren. Eric Matthews survives a terrible car accident only to find out everyone in town thinks he's a murderer—and he has to clear his name even though he has no memories of what happened. (978-1-60282-214-6)

Mesmerized by David-Matthew Barnes. Through her close friendship with Brodie and Lance, Serena Albright learns about the many forms of love and finds comfort for the grief and guilt she feels over the brutal death of her older brother, the victim of a hate crime. (978-1-60282-191-0)

The Perfect Family by Kathryn Shay. A mother and her gay son stand hand in hand as the storms of change engulf their perfect family and the life they knew. (978-1-60282-181-1)

Father Knows Best by Lynda Sandoval. High school juniors and best friends Lila Moreno, Meryl Morganstern, and Caressa Thibodoux plan to make the most of the summer before senior year. What they discover that amazing summer about girl power, growing up, and trusting friends and family more than prepares them to tackle that all-important senior year! (978-1-60282-147-7)